Books by Larry M. Greer

Soft Target

Heaven is in Union County

Soft Target

Larry M. Greer

This is a work of fiction. Names, characters, places and incidents either are the product of the author's imagination or are used fictitiously. Any resemblance to actual persons living or dead, events, or locales is entirely coincidental.

ISBN-13: 978-1505630725

ISBN-10: 150563072X

Cover design by Amanda Phillips
Book Design by Karin Corbeil

Published and Printed
in the United States of America 2015

Dedication

This book is dedicated in loving memory of my wife of nearly 57 years, Maxine Martin Greer.

Acknowledgements

I wish to thank Carol HasBrouck for the many hours she spent line-editing my story. Being a stickler for detail, she and I spent many hours reworking the dialog.

In order to put the book between two covers I relied on Karin "Casey" Corbeil to use her skills to bring it all together into book form. Thank you Casey, for being there for me.

And my two friends, Mike Royster and Gloria Ipock who took the time to read my draft and gave me encouragement to finish the book.

Larry M. Greer

Soft Target

Foreword

Make no mistake! If you do not support our jihadist cause, you will be killed! America, as you know it, will no longer exist, for our mission is to dominate the world!

Let me introduce myself. I am Mohamed. I am from Jiba, a small village in Northern Pakistan. This story is about the last ten years of my life.

I am the son of a poor shepherd, whose family lives in extreme poverty. Although I come from a very ordinary circumstance, I am an extraordinary boy! I possess very high intelligence and unlike many of your American boys, I have applied this intelligence to my schooling. You should be fearful of my education, as I now join many other young men from my part of the world who are trained jihadist killers with a passion for fulfilling Allah's mission. Be warned, for just as on September 11, 2001, you and your kind are my target!

Mohamed of Jiba

Soft Target
by Larry Greer

PROLOGUE

Northern Pakistan

BaaRooommmmmm ----- BaaRooommmmmm --- the deep moaning sound of the ancient sheep horn reverberated up the mountain slopes through the damp fog that draped like a shroud over the valley below. Wrapped snugly in my sheep skin blankets, I slept soundly on thick mountain grass. I had tucked my canvas tent between two large boulders. Even at five thousand feet on the top of the Guru Mountain Range of Northern Pakistan, I was quite well protected from the frigid wind and icy rain. The blaring sheep horn finally roused me from my morning sleep. Daylight would mean the first of five daily prayers to Allah. I reluctantly rolled over and stumbled to a small stream flowing out from beneath a large boulder. I washed my face in the icy water, and stumbled back to where I had rolled out my prayer rug. I dropped down on my knees, facing east toward Mecca to recite my morning prayers. The sun had not fully crested the distant mountains, and together they created the purple and orange hues of dawn.

As long as I could remember, my father had been a sheepherder. In recent years his knees had begun to ache due to many years of tending our flock in the bitterly cold winters. Now, even in the spring, climbing the steep slopes to the warm grassy meadows where our flock would remain from the first of May until the last days of August had become almost unbearable. Some years, beginning as early as September, it would become too cold

Soft Target
by Larry Greer

for a shepherd of any age to survive without substantial shelter so their sheep had to be driven back down into the valley. Because of these conditions, tending the flock on the high mountain slopes had now become primarily my job. Once a week, my younger brother, Hasped, would make the steep climb from our tiny village of Jiba to visit me. I was the oldest son, so naturally the job of tending the family sheep fell to me. Our little village in Northern Pakistan was located almost one hundred miles west of the town of Taxila. Hasped would bring me food and always some new reading material. These were usually on loan from the local Madrassas School. I also got clean clothes that my mother had tucked into his satchel. He would spend one night with me and we warmed ourselves around the small fire and talked into the wee hours of the night. He would share news of the village. I treasured this time alone with my brother. He came bearing the delicious local fruit and freshly baked bread, but what I hungered for most, was new reading material. There were few newspapers in Jiba. Most were left by people passing through from the big cities. I read everything I could get my hands on. I had always been a quick learner and at 9 years old I could read as well as most adults in my village. I did not know it then, but my 14th year, would be my last summer caring for the flock. Village elders were making secret arrangements to change my life. I would leave the village for some kind of special training at a camp in neighboring Afghanistan.

Tending sheep was a lonely job, far from my little village and my family and my friends. I missed playing street games with my friends in the late afternoons. It was lonely up here. Only occasionally would I run into another shepherd. I could see him on a distant slope and we would come together and talk around the evening campfire.

Hasped had departed early this morning for the village. After my prayers and a breakfast of soft bread, fresh cheese and

Soft Target
by Larry Greer

figs, I pulled out the cherished reading material from Hasped's bag. He had brought two books, along with a couple of newspapers.

As I descended the mountain at the end of August, I knew this would mean school would begin soon. What I didn't know, was that I had been chosen to take series of special tests at my school. As always, I achieved high scores. Because of these scores, I was singled from out of all the other children in my village for special tutoring in both English and Spanish. My father explained that I was very privileged to get the opportunity to learn foreign languages, and admonished me to do my studies and not ask questions. I was to focus on excelling in these two subjects. My father was not a forceful man and had an almost fearful respect for authority. I knew better than to question his directive.

Even at 13, I was small for my age, and by no means muscular. My only physical skill was running. I could out-run almost anyone in school. However, my intellect compensated for my physical shortcomings. Schoolwork had always come easy and I was usually at the top of my class in all subjects. For this I was chided and envied by my classmates.

One day a village elder took my father aside. He whispered that I must begin building my strength, for I would need it in the near future. He told my father that I would be leaving for a special school in the fall of my 15th year. The elder went on to tell my father that our country was at war with "the infidels" to the West, and I had been chosen for special training. It was for that reason that I was being tutored in English and Spanish. My father was astounded, but proud. The elder continued by admonishing my father to keep this information confidential. If my father ever divulged any part of this conversation, the penalty could result in death for us both. In addition, and my mother and brother would be banished from the village and shunned by our people. At this point, I was then called in and the elder spoke directly to me as he repeated the admonishments.

"Am I making myself clear Mohamad?"
"Yes Elder, I understand". I was both afraid and excited.
"Elder, may I ask a question?" I ventured. I could see my father's disapproving look, but I persisted.

"I am the eldest son and my father is not well. He needs me to tend our herd. My younger brother is not yet old enough to take my place, so how are they to manage with me gone?" The elder was firm. "Mohamad, your family will be taken care of in your absence. Where you are going, you will not need an income. And your every need will be provided."

"Elder, where am I going and what purpose will I serve Allah?"

"I cannot answer either of your questions, Mohamad. Know only that you are a very special young man, singled out to serve our people in a time when the infidels are threatening our way of life. They must be defeated, and you, Mohamad, are destined to play an important role in our victory. You must praise Allah for this honor!"

Soft Target
by Larry Greer

CHAPTER I

2002 Northern Pakistan

When I was 14 years old, I remembered very well the day a man on horseback came to our village. I heard my father say that there was going to be to be an important meeting so, being curious, I scurried to the village meeting house. I slipped in and hid under a cloth-draped table. Anytime a visitor brought news from the city, it was a momentous occasion.

Because of my diminutive size I had no problem hiding under the table. Soon the elders began to filter in. Some placed wine, fruit and bread, on the table I was hiding under. I could see their feet merely inches from my face, and perspiration began to run down my cheek. I feared they could hear my heart pounding loudly in my chest.

Once the elders were seated on the floor, the visitor began to speak. He talked about a fearless leader name Osama bin Laden, who had struck a mighty blow to the Western infidels in America, and bragged that thousands had been killed. The elders murmured in unison: "praise be to Allah". The visitor went on saying that bin Laden was now looking for brave young men to join him in this Jihad. There had been a search for the most intelligent in each village. These boys with many others would be specially trained to help wipe out the infidels.

Soft Target
by Larry Greer

The meeting was long, and the temperature under the table was stifling, yet I remained still and quiet. I only vaguely understood what was being discussed. Never did I imagine I would be part of the group that bin Laden was going to organize. Several spoke of airplanes. This was a curiosity for me. I had seen some photos of airplanes but had never a real plane. I had, however, watched the white streaks' high in the sky that my father claimed were the tailings from of large airplanes I longed to set my eyes on one for myself. After what seemed like hours, the elders stood and thanked the visitor. At this time they approached the table where I hid to partake of the wine, fruit and bread. I was petrified, too afraid to even breathe. I needed desperately to go outside and relieve myself. They continued to converse, moving around the table. They seemed to talk forever, but finally the last elder left the building.

Despite my young age, I understood the importance of this meeting. The next day I would find the globe at my school to see where this "America" was in relationship to my village. At school they taught us to hate the infidels, yet I did not quite understand why. As time went on, I also began to adopt hatred of an enemy I was yet to know. I learned much later, that only a small percentage of schools taught this hatred of the Western infidels, and they were usually located in small isolated villages like mine. My routine at school consisted of prayer time on my rug, memorization of the Quran, and my English and Spanish studies along with the rest of my classes. Because learning came so easy, boredom carried my mind to places beyond my small village. I longed to do more than study about the world. Little did I know how soon I would get my wish.

Two weeks had passed since the stranger's visit and commotion over his news was unrelenting among the village elders. Then word began to spread that a special test would be given to all 13 and 14 year-old boys. Everyone in our small village of five hundred was excited and curious. What would happen for those boys who passed the test? Fifty-four boys fell into that age range and I was one of them. The morning of the test my adrenalin was flowing. My father set his hand on my arm and admonished me not to worry. He was confident I would have top scores as I always did. That morning, the boys were divided into three groups. We would be sequentially tested in math, English and a review of the Quran. This news increased my anxiety, as I was at the top of my class in math. My English was improving, but here I was not as confident. At that time, English was an accepted language in Pakistan and was spoken by about fifty percent of people in the large cities. But Jiba was a small remote village and everyone spoke either the Urdu or Shina language. Very few spoke English.

  The test was long, but I ran home feeling confident that I had done well, even in English. I washed and put on clean clothes as was the custom before the noon prayer. At the completion of my prayers, I joined the family for our noon meal. My mother noted my smile and asked about the tests. Cautiously, I told them I thought I had done well and that my English studies had given me an advantage on that test and the math and Quran seemed easy. Mother was openly proud, but my always-cautious father, "hoped that I was not being too boastful." That night, Hasped and I talked long into the night, theorizing what all this could mean for me and for our country.

CHAPTER 2

The Elder's Visit

Two weeks had passed and none of us who had taken the test had heard anything about our results. Late that night, I heard a knock on our door. My father answered the door. He quickly stepped outside and closed it behind him. Hasped and I exchanged glances, both wondering if this visitor would bring answers about my test scores. Moments later my father came back inside and informed me that I was to go with him the next day to the village hall to meet with two of the elders.

"Father, what is this all about"? I queried.
"Mohamed, you must be patient. Tomorrow all will be revealed.

The next morning it seemed to take forever to complete our morning routine. Finally, my father motioned that he was ready to head to the meeting house. I was on edge and all my senses were ripe. Heavy rain had persisted all night, creating large muddy puddles for us to maneuver. The drainage ditches were overflowing, and the stench of sewage was pungent in the air. This was a familiar smell, and one I hated. To me it represented the smell of poverty.

Jiba was an extremely poor village, and yet we were happy. It was a simple life. We grew our own food, wove our cloth and traded handmade goods with nearby villages. The few families who owned a refrigerator were considered wealthy. Most homes

Soft Target
by Larry Greer

did not have more than one power outlet for which they paid the government one hundred Rupees. My family was better off than many due to our sizable herd of sheep. Counting the twelve spring lambs, we had forty-four head this year. My father sheared the wool twice a year, which my mother used to weave rugs which she sold in Taxila. The milk was used to make butter for bartering and on very special occasions, like a wedding or the death of a beloved elder, we would slaughter a lamb.

  Father and I entered the meeting house. It was empty with the exception of two elders who were sitting cross-legged on a floor that was covered by many colorful rugs. The shutters had been opened on opposite walls, allowing a light breeze to wander through the room. I caught a whiff of the sewage smell and shuddered. Although I sensed this meeting was about me, I knew enough to keep behind my father. As was the custom, he offered a subtle bow to the elders. He stepped aside and indicated I should offer my bow, as well. The first elder gestured for us to sit in front of them. He offered tea for my father from the tray set before them. My father accepted the tea and nodded thanks. I was still considered a child so was not offered tea. The second elder, after taking several sips of his tea, cleared his throat. Speaking directly to my father, he revealed that we were meeting as a result of my test scores from two weeks before. According to the officials from the Madrassas schools in the village of Jiba and Taxila, had determined the most outstanding students from the testing. Much consideration was given to math and the memorizing of the Quran. The English scores were considered a bonus.

  I listened, willing my wildly beating heart to be silent. Although my facial expression never changed, my stomach churned and the anxiety made me nauseous.
Suddenly, the second elder looked directly at me and spoke.

Soft Target
by Larry Greer

"Mohamed, you are very young, but very intelligent, therefore, I know you will understand what I have to say. You may not be aware, but Allah's Al-Qaeda Army struck a mighty blow against the Western infidels on September 11th 2001. The leaders of our army know that the infidels will be anxious to strike back. The infidels are a confident and mighty force to reckon with, but Allah is great, and because he is on our side, we can bring the infidels to their knees. Many of their leaders are cowards and make many decisions out of greed. They will want to withdraw their armies from the lands of Islam in order to appease their people. These traits bring them unwittingly into our leader's hands. If you have studied history as well as you have math and the Quran, you will remember many great armies in ancient history have fallen because of corruption and greed. That history is now repeating itself in America as well as in Europe. All this is happening as I speak to you, Mohamed. They are so misguided that they now even search old women for weapons in their airports. Our people know these things for they follow the American media and stay in touch with our brothers in the United States through the internet. This leads me Mohamed, to tell you why you have been privileged to come to this meeting.

"You took a test several weeks ago and competed with boys your age both here in Jiba as well as in Taxila. Mohamad, you did exceedingly well in math and did not make any mistakes in the test about the Quran. You were average in the English test, but that was not the most important part. Your teachers highly recommended you for advancement. Out of all the young men your age, you, Mohamad, your scores are the highest and you are the first choice of the selection committee."

I looked up at my father, but his face was stoic. He revealed no sign of happiness or pride.
The elder went on:

Soft Target
by Larry Greer

"Mohamad, this next fall after you come down from the mountains with your father's sheep, you will report to a special Madrassas school in Taxila. There you will receive special training in English and Spanish as well as classes in computers and the familiarity with the internet. You will come home to your family for one week every three months. In the fall of the year after your sixteenth birthday, you will be sent to a special camp where you will continue serving Allah. Is all this understood?"
I could feel tiny tears forming in the back of my eyes, but I was determined to contain my composure. After all, I was being addressed as an adult, was I not?

"Yes Elder, I understand and I am honored to have been chosen."

The second elder made one last comment.
"Mohamad, you are mature beyond your age."

That night after Hasped had gone to sleep, I cried myself to sleep.

CHAPTER 3

The Madrassas School

I was now well into my first year at the Madrassas School in Taxila. I was learning many new things. Much of what I learned was beyond my comprehension: cell phones, television, computers, the internet. Before coming to this school, I had never even used a telephone, or a computer, and the internet was a total wonder. I quickly took to playing computer war games. This activity was useful in my training as well as fun, as it taught me to be quick and decisive. Because of my small stature, I had avoided team sports with the boys in Jiba, well, except stick ball. Here, I was taught baseball and learned to swim. Boxing was not a favorite, but I was instructed to participate because I would be introduced to far more advance self-defense tactics within the next couple of years.

During those years at the Madrassas School, I read everything I could get my hands on. One day I found an old newspaper, torn and tattered on the edges. It caught my attention, as the headline screamed: 'ARABS BOMB NEW YORK, in big bold letters. The date was September 11, 2001. This information put our classroom instruction into greater focus.

I had made friends with two boys who had started at the same time I had. When no one else was within earshot, we would speculate on what kind of camp we would be going to when we turned nineteen. One of the boys was named Raga. He was sure we would be joining the army, but did not understand how what we were learning at this Madrassas, had anything to do with the army. Learning Spanish was truly a mystery to him. None of us had ever seen a Hispanic person and could not understand the benefit of speaking this strange language. Johey, was the other boys name. He had come from a wealthy family and talked like he knew more about our fate than we did. But in reality, he had no more knowledge than Raga or me.

The teachers spent a lot of time teaching us about Europe and America and why we should fear and hate these Western infidels. We were fed a daily diet of the evils of Western culture, capitalism and Christianity. They drilled into us that we must be prepared to defend Islam. We did not dare ask *why* the infidels were our enemies. We knew our job was to merely be obedient.

During the spring of 2003, during our second year, the headmaster herded all the students into a big meeting room and informed us that the infidels from America had just attacked Bagdad in Iraq. He turned the TV to the CNN station and to our amazement we were watching the attack live! We were in shock as we watched the large night time explosions across the city of Bagdad. There was silence among us for the next couple of hours. The headmaster drew Johey and Raga and I into a separate room.

"This is what you are being trained for. Someday, you will serve Allah and protect Islam from these infidels."

Still we did not understand how our training was connected to a war in the far off land of Iraq. But custom dictated, we remained quiet and obedient.

The news was followed up the next day in class by the teachers, who covered in great detail, the country of Iraq, someone called Saddam Hussein and the Americans evil. It was rumored that Iraq possessed very powerful weapons, capable of unbelievable destruction and might even use them against other

Soft Target
by Larry Greer

Arab countries like Pakistan. Teachers explained that Saddam Hussein was no friend of Pakistan. He had already killed thousands of his own countrymen known as Kurds. They were killed with a lethal poison called Saran gas. We were told that Pakistan was safe from Iraq because they were armed with a weapon much more powerful, which the teachers referred to as "nuclear weapons." Part of our instruction that day included the irony of history. We learned about how the Americans actually partnered with a group called Mujahideen to defeat the Russians, who were invading Afghanistan in 1980's. Ironically, a portion of that underground army is now Al-Qaeda, an avowed enemy of America.

  In our third year, after concentrated English classes, most of the boys were proficient enough in the language to understand American TV. Teachers encouraged the boys to watch CNN and pointed out how the media in America shared government secrets. This information was becoming very helpful to their enemies. Because what we heard on television was so foreign to our teaching, we had many questions. The teachers were adamant that lack of control over the media would be America's downfall. They instilled in us that infidels were stupid. Even though the American President had declared war on Islam after the bombings of 2001, we were told that Islam would be victorious and Allah would rule. Somewhere in Afghanistan or even in our own province of Northern Pakistan, Osama bin Laden was training boys only slightly older than us in tactics to crush the Western infidels.

  It was 2006 and I was turning 18. A daily diet of hatred was being pounded into my head. As we were sheltered in our Madrassas School, the world was changing around us. Only two years earlier, the city of Bagdad, Iraq, had been consumed by a bloody battle. Over one hundred thousand troops, mostly Americans, invaded the city, and the Iraqi Army dissolved into the

Soft Target
by Larry Greer

general population, becoming guerilla fighters. This War in Iraq had a profound impact on my psyche.

I began to form strong opinions of my own about the infidels. We were becoming fighters. Target practice was a daily ritual. Each day I looked forward to cradling my rifle at my shoulder and shooting the paper infidel targets. One day, I suddenly realized what I wanted was the opportunity to kill the real enemy. I had become an expert marksman. I was good...really good! I proudly wore a pro- marksman badge on my shirt. I longed for my father to see how well I was doing. He would be proud of me. Even as young as 18, I began to develop leadership skills. I did not realize until much later, that I was distancing myself from Raga and Johey. My military and leadership skills were impacting my attitude. Unconsciously, I had begun to feel superior to my fellow students and even to my friends. In what little free time we had, I devoured books about famous war heroes of history. I was consumed by stories of Genghis Khan and the famous Chinese General, Sun Tzu. I studied their leadership styles and battle strategies. As the year progressed, teachers began to notice my maturity and how serious and focused I had become. They wrote glowing reports that were being passed on to leaders unknown even to the Madrassas School. I was also maturing physically. I was tall and although lean, I was still very muscular. As I neared my 19th birthday, I followed the customs of my people and grew a beard. I was told that I had sharp facial features and my black eyes made me appear fierce. The fact that I almost never smiled, enhanced this image. I was becoming anxious to move...to truly become a freedom fighter...a Mujahideen and now more appropriately a Taliban.

CHAPTER 4

2006 – Transitions

Shortly before my 19th birthday I had been allowed to spend a month at home with my family. My mother and father could see changes in me they did not like. It did not please them that I was distant and preoccupied. My brother, Hasped also felt the change in me and badgered me to talk about the school and what I had been taught, but I knew I could not talk about it. At the end of the visit as I was saying my good byes, I felt tears swell in my eyes as I hugged my mother goodbye. It was the only tender emotion I had allowed myself to feel in years.

Very late, one cold winter night, back in my room at school, I was startled by a knock on my door. Standing there was the headmaster. Behind him, in the dim light of early morning, was a man I had never seen. He was about 45 and his face was utterly expressionless. He wore military clothing and boots. The Madrassas' headmaster spoke.
"Mohamad, the time has come for you to leave our school and move on to the second phase of your training. Quickly gather your clothes and belongings and follow him". He pointed to the second man. No words were spoken. He silently stood and waited for me. Anticipation gripped my chest. This was it. This was my chance to become a freedom fighter.

I threw my meager belongings into my pack and moments later later the three of us walked down the dimly lit hall. Upon reaching the door leading outside the building, I turned to the

Soft Target
by Larry Greer

headmaster and bowed. I thanked him for his teachings over the past four years. He only replied that he prayed for Allah to be with me. It was very dark at 2:00am and raining. A van was waiting and as I climbed aboard I saw that Raga and Johey were already in the van. The man who we did not yet know got in the back with us and closed the door. Still no words were spoken. Raga and Johey and I looked at each other with both excitement and trepidation, but none of us had the courage to speak. The driver of the van was just as mysterious. He looked straight ahead, and we only saw part of his face as he pulled a black curtain across the van none of us could see out the windshield. It was then that I noticed that the side windows were also blacked out. We were sitting in total darkness and freezing cold. The only benefit was that we were no longer in the rain. No one said a word as the van navigated the pot holes of a road that had not been paved in decades. After almost an hour, the man sitting with us said:

"My name is Rallhas and I will soon learn your strengths. If you are worthy, we will become friends...over time. It is my duty to escort you and others like you. You have been selected and trained for several reasons...because you are intelligent and dedicated to Allah. The other reasons will be explained to you at a later time by our leader. You have learned much over the past five years, but there is much more to be learned. Some of it will be from books, but much of it will come from real life field training. If you are wondering why you cannot see out of this van, it is because our destination is secret. I will not tell you more, so do not ask. The location of our camp is known to only a few and you will understand all as time goes on. The trip will take three days and three nights. It is not a comfortable journey. During that time, you will only leave the van when I tell you. If you need to relieve yourself, I have placed a jar under your seat. We will travel only at night so early in the morning we will pull into a building where we will spend our time until after dark tomorrow night. I will not talk

Soft Target
by Larry Greer

to you of future plans, so do not ask. I have brought reading material as well as some cards for your amusement."

Just before daylight, I was awakened as the van bumped onto an unpaved and rutted road. The ride was bumpy and the van swerved with frequent turns. After thirty minutes the van stopped and the driver cracked his window and spoke in low tones to someone standing near the van. I could not hear what was being said, but after a few minutes I heard metal grinding. The van began to slowly roll again and then the pavement felt smooth. The van stopped, and the metal grinding sound could again be heard behind us. The driver opened his door and came around to open the van's side door. Rallhas was the first to get out and motioned for the three of us to follow. We gingerly stepped out of the van. Our eyes were not accustomed to light and our legs were cramped. I could see that we were inside of some kind of cinderblock warehouse. There were no windows, so we had no way to gauge the time of day. The only furnishings in the bare warehouse were five sweat-stained cots and two naked light bulbs swinging from long frayed cords. Rallhas spoke:

"This is going to be your home for today, so I suggest that you use the facilities and prepare for your morning prayers. East is that direction." He pointed. "After prayers, food will be set on that table." He pointed. "If you are tired from your night in the van, you should consider taking a rest on your cot. I brought along cards, as I said, or you can read the newspapers I laid out on the table. My companion and I are under strict orders not to tell you where you are in relation to the camp. This is for your own protection. Should you be captured in the future, you would not be able to identify our camp location."

I could no longer contain my curiosity. "Is there nothing that you can tell us about the camp or what we can expect when we get there?" Rallhas responded a little impatiently, "Mohamed, you will have plenty of time after we get to the camp to learn all you need to know. This lack of information, again, is for your protection."

I nodded, acknowledging that I understood but thought to myself, "Why is it necessary to keep everything so secret?"

On the third night of traveling, we stopped somewhere far out in the country side. I had noticed that I had not seen on-coming traffic or village lights along the road for many hours. Rallhas said that they had come as far as we could by van so other transportation was prepared to take us the rest of the way.

"All right," Rallhas said, "Before getting out of the van, I want each of you to put the hoods that I am handing you over your heads. You will not see the way into the camp which is still some distant away."

The three of us said nothing, but did as we were told. Rallhas took each one individually by the arm and helped us out of the van. Raga whispered quietly to me, "I think we will be walking the rest of the way." However, he was wrong. Once we were all standing beside the van, Rallhas laughed, "Ever ridden a donkey? Ok, Mohamed, step up and I will put your foot in the stirrup, and you can then throw your right leg over, and you will be sitting on a Jack Ass. All you have to do is hold onto the saddle. The donkeys will all be tethered to each other. I will ride the first one and be the leader. If you don't understand my directions, say something now." No one spoke. "Good, we have about a six-hour ride, so I suggest if you need to go, you should do it now."

I was thinking how well planned this trip had been and continued to ponder the reason for such secrecy. I ascended to the back of the donkey without much trouble, but my confidence fled

Soft Target
by Larry Greer

when my animal started to move forward. I prayed to Allah that this beast would be as sure-footed as his reputation.

Eventually I picked up the rhythm of his gait. I listened as the sound the van become more distant. Perhaps the driver was going back to Taxila. After an hour or more I could tell we had moved into the mountains. I felt a slight chill to the air and the changing gait of the donkey as he picked his way up a path of loose rocks. Nearby, I could hear water rushing over rocks. We were not used to riding, and our back sides began to ache. By this time, we knew better than to either ask questions or complain. I did not know what Johey or Raga thought about all this intrigue, but it excited me, and I looked forward to my new adventure. After climbing for about two hours, the air became dramatically cooler and I could tell by crunch of the donkeys' hooves that we were crossing snow-covered ground. Because of my sheep-herding days, I was familiar with this kind of high country. So, I assumed that we would eventually reach a mountain pass and finally traverse down into a valley. I was correct. We began to descend rather quickly. I could tell it was steep as the donkeys slowly and deliberate placed each hoof. As I predicted, we reached more level ground and the flattened path created a much easier journey. Rallhas shouted back that we were almost at the camp. I could hear a deep voice resonating in the distance. It sounded like someone giving orders. We continued a ways further and suddenly the deep voice was right beside us. "Hey Rallhas, I see you are back and have brought some fresh meat with you."
This comment was followed by the laughter of several other voices, also standing nearby.
"Oh yes, I have brought some fine new recruits. The Commander will be pleased," responded Rallhas.

Much to my dismay, this interaction between the men did not prove to be the end of our journey. The donkeys again started to move. After about 10 minutes their hoofs struck a harder

Soft Target
by Larry Greer

surface creating yet a different sound. Even the air had a different smell. The odor of wood smoke permeated my nose and accompanied something wonderful...the smell of food cooking. Finally I could hear Rallhas.

"Alright men, you may lift your hoods. You are now in the Commander's camp." It took me a few minutes to adjust my eyes, after removing the suffocating hood. What I saw was amazing. Before me was a huge concrete structure. It was topped with a thick earth-covered roof containing live shrubs as camouflage. With my eyes still unused to the light, I squinted into the opening and it appeared to enclose a small village. We entered as a group and saw small rooms encircling the interior walls. The center of the compound was an open arena. A small stream flowed through the center. As we were absorbing this compound, the deep voice from earlier, startled us. "Welcome, recruits." Raga, Johey and I spun around to find that the voice belonged to a scar-faced man. His head was devoid of hair, with the exception of a bushy mustache. His stern countenance and sharp, deep voice made it hard to look him directly in his face. Utilizing that deep, gruff voice, he admonished, "When you address me, you will stand at attention and will salute. Is that understood?"

The Madrassas School had not taught the three boys about the harsh disciplines of the army. They were clueless about how they were expected to conduct themselves. Mohamed took the lead. He had a premonition about what they would experience. He clicked his heels. The other two followed his lead. All three did as the gruff-voiced man instructed. They stood as tall as they could and saluted. The man laughed and said
"Not bad for a first attempt, but not correct. If you are to survive, I expect you to learn quickly what is expected of you from the daily drills. You will learn there are several of us in charge. You will not address us by title or see ranks on our clothing. You will learn that the infidels use this against us. You are the first of twelve new recruits. The rest will be here soon. When you address me, you

must call me Valdess." He turned to Rallhas and instructed, "These boys are not accustomed to our training. They are probably tired from their little trip. Take them to their bunks. They must be rested and ready for morning prayers."

Valdess sharply turned to the three boys and said, "After morning prayers you will eat. After noon prayers you will report to the 'S' block." He abruptly turned and left. Rallhas continued the introduction to camp for the boys. "This stream is our only source of water. Do not forget this instruction. The stream above the stone is for drinking. The water below the stone is for bathing and nothing else. Outside the building is for washing your clothes. You will never wash your clothes in the daytime. The only washing of clothes will be after dark. You will wash them quickly and return to your bunk areas. Hang your clothes near you to dry. Never leave anything outside of this compound. It must not be obvious that this valley is occupied in any way."

I noticed that the compound had round holes in the roof that allowed for plenty of light. I would later understand that the shrubs and grass on the roof provided a camouflage. The holes in the roof, providing for light, could not be detected from the air as sky lights. The compound was dimly lit at night by a gas generator. Few lights were allowed, to keep detection to a minimum. We were directed to our bunks. With so much to take in, none of us slept well. The next day came very early. After morning prayers Rallhas told us new recruits that we were fortunate to appear first, as they would be lenient today. The remaining recruits would not be in camp until some time that night. He then took a few minutes to tell us in general, what we could expect.

"First, if you are in this building at the time of prayer, you will notice that the Qibla is on the southeast wall, pointing you East toward Mecca. You will wash your selves in the lower stream before all prayers. I assume you remember your instructions from

Soft Target
by Larry Greer

last night. Having done that you will join your team of twelve in the designated area for what we call the 'S'cell, meaning special team. There are eighty-eight other recruits, already here and in various stages of training. Most of them are older and seasoned members of the Commanders group. You should expect to be bullied. This is normal for new recruits. If you are to be successful, you cannot let them bother you. It's all part of toughing you up for what is ahead. You will be experiencing very rigorous combat exercises and through daily target practice, you will be expected to become top marksmen. Your food will be high in calories to aid in building your muscle mass to your full potential. You will be given one hour of rest after noon prayers and will have time to yourselves after evening prayers. As you already know, our camp location is extremely secret. Do not waste time speculating with each other about where you are. Doing so, will be dangerous to your health. There will be no communications outside of this camp, except through our commander. There is outdoor training at night several times a week and if we train outside the camp in the daytime, it is because we have very carefully calculated the movement of our enemy's satellites. You will be advised in much more detail on all you will experience."

Soft Target
by Larry Greer

CHAPTER 5

The Camp

Day three was a full agenda. The other nine recruits in our group had arrived and were rested. In all, there were over one hundred soldiers and a staff of twelve. The first time Raga, Johey and I saw them all together was that morning at dawn, when we gathered to say morning prayers. Then on signal, they all went to individual squares on the indoor field. The twelve of us new recruits had been given uniforms, and boots. To be in this camp, among trained soldiers and other recruits, made me feel like a grown man for the first time in my 18 plus short years. Although Raga, Johey and I had all received the same teaching, I was invigorated and excited. Raga and Johey appeared to be more nervous than anything else.

There was a hush on the field as Valdess stepped onto a small platform. He turned his head up toward the sky. He began, "Praise to Allah. He then addressed all the soldiers. Our new recruits have arrived. They are delivered into the hands of our commander. They will be trained to serve Allah in this very special unit. They come to us as the brightest and best from throughout our country. You will welcome them to our service." There was a loud hurrah from all but the twelve new recruits. His voice changing to one of a somber tone, "I have some unfortunate news to report this morning. Six of our unit's members were killed in the Philippines two weeks ago, and last week, ten were captured in London. They were in the process of boarding planes to New York and Washington, but unfortunately, they grew careless. Let this be a lesson. We cannot be too careful. Our successes, praise Allah, have caused our enemies to intensify the search for our brothers. But remember, we are many and we grow stronger every day."

Given the secretive nature of this camp, Mohamad wondered how they had received the news, but guessed that someone like Rallhas might have reported it from the outside.

The morning began with the rigorous combat exercises that Rallhas had warned them about. All commands were given in English. Raja and Johey turned to Mohammed with a surprised look on their face. Mohammed was not surprised. In fact, he expected that they would also provide some instruction in Spanish. He would not be disappointed. That day, his "S-cell" was instructed to speak only English or Spanish. He surmised that the purpose was to sharpen their skills and remove their accent. At first, it was awkward, but eventually it became very natural.

Several days later, Mohammed's special recruit unit was told that they would be taking a tour outside the building. Based on their initial information, this surprised the twelve boys. From nowhere, Rallhas appeared to take charge of the tour. "This is important, so listen carefully. Our training exercise outside the compound, will take place between 1:28pm and 2:48pm this afternoon. This time is critical, as there will be no enemy spy satellites over our region at that time. We have precisely eighty minutes to complete our training and get inside our compound without being detected. This is very different from the training we do during the night and much more dangerous. Are there any questions?"

Raga spoke up and hesitantly asked,
"Can the satellites really see us on the ground from that far up in the sky?"

Soft Target
by Larry Greer

"Yes. Our enemy's satellites are very powerful, Raga." responded Rallhas. This information was not easy for the recruits to digest, but they accepted it as truth, just as they accepted all they were taught as truth. After performing maneuvers in the camouflage-covered field outside the compound's walls, they scurried back inside the camp. Rallhas continued his instruction.

"You will now see the classrooms where you will begin your work. Your special unit will be spending many hours together in these rooms. Each room has a unique number and a different class will be taught in each room. Let's start by learning what will be taught in Room #1."

I noticed that there were boxes on each of the tables. Large black devices were placed atop the boxes.

"What we have here" Rollhas continued, "is called a short-wave radio. It is not new technology, but very useful. You will learn how to talk back and forth with each other on these radios. Their unique purpose in our technology tools is their ability to operate undetected. They run a low radio frequency which is very difficult for our enemies to observe. Another very important tool represents much newer technology. These are cellular phones. As you carry out your mission for Allah, these cellular phones will be invaluable. Unfortunately, they are of no use here and one of their drawbacks is that our enemies can listen in on our every word. You will learn more about the cell phone and its uses nearer the end of your time here in camp. As far as the short wave radios, you will be expected to know how to use them, how to take them completely apart and how to re-assemble them. Do not ask questions. Our purpose will become clear as you go through your training."

Soft Target
by Larry Greer

Some of the new recruits who came to the camp from larger cities were familiar with the cell phones, but Mohamed, Johey and Raga were not. This new technology mystified them.

Rollhas continued, "The Classroom #2 is the largest room and one where you will spend much time. It is where you will learn to build explosives…many different types of explosive devises. The instructors in this class are the best in the world. When your time is complete here, you will be experts at constructing and deconstructing many types of explosive devises."

If Mohamad and his two friends had any second thoughts about why they were here at this camp, it was too late. They were now on a path that would determine their destiny. Any sign that they were questioning their purpose would mean certain death, probably with a bullet to the head.

Rallhas continued his tour of the classrooms,

"Classroom #3 is our computer laboratory. Here everyone will be required to learn in great detail how to extract and manipulate information critical for your mission. You will also learn about, but not use the internet. It is not safe in our location. Every piece of information about locations critical to your mission will be provided on small transportable electronic devices. You will be expected to thoroughly study all this information. Each of you will be given your own computer. Once you arrive at your mission site, it is safe to begin utilizing information from the worldwide internet.

Finally, Classroom #4 is what we call the code room. Here you will be taught very critical skill. You will be communicating with each other using ordinary English conversation, but by inserting words into your discussion that that mean something else entirely, this code process will allow you communicate vital information that will not be understood by our enemy. Praise Allah, so far, this code system has been successful worldwide."

CHAPTER 6

Training of a Terrorist

On the morning of the fifth day of training, the 'S' cell recruits were called, to a special meeting in a room adjacent to Valdess' living quarters. The room was different than any other they had seen. It as carpeted, as were most Pakistani meeting rooms. But there the similarity stopped. Blackboards surrounded the walls on two sides. The other two walls contained maps of the world. As was the custom, shoes were not in any room with carpet, so boots were removed and slippers were made available. Rallhas directed us to sit, as we customarily did, cross-legged on the floor. Valdess was expected soon. Johey leaned over to me and whispered,

"What do you think we are here for?"

"I don't know, but I suspect this is very important to our mission." I suggested that he had better listen very closely and take notes, as I planned to do. I continued, "I guarantee, they will not repeat any of this information so let's pay attention and tell Raga as well."

Moments later Valdess came in and stood before them. His face communicated that he would be sharing both serious and important information.

Soft Target
by Larry Greer

"Good morning---- you have now received four days of orientation to our camp. If you have questions, now would be the time to ask." As I suspected, there was deadly silence.

"Good," Valdess continued. "Rallhas has obviously done his job well. Now is the time for you to learn the true purpose of your training. I have been told that some of you have been asking questions. Being well trained is critical to our success. So by all means, ask questions. However, you are never to question our purpose. Is that clear?" Again, deadly silence.

"Let me give you some history. Before what is now known as "Nine Eleven," the Commander put together the first 'S' cell made up of eighteen top-notch soldiers. They trained in a camp very much like this one, but at that time, because we had not yet alerted the infidel's to our purpose, the first "S-cell" team trained in the open and freely learned to use all the communication devices without fear of discovery. In all of Pakistan's history, it was one of the most strategically planned attacks ever made on foreign soil. With the exception of one, the remainders of the 18 brothers are now with Allah. As Arabs, we have chosen this path because it is clear that the infidels are set on imposing their evil beliefs on our world. They need our oil and their armies are on a path to total domination. They have infiltrated into both Iraq and Afghanistan. Because of their aggression, we have lost many soldiers. But we have grown wise to their tactics and we now have a secret presence in many parts of their world. They fear us and they should, as many of our people are secretly working in their country. They have suspicions about our presence and have named our soldiers 'sleeper cells'. As I said, we have become wise to their tactics and have not been detected. At a signal from our Commander, our soldiers are ready to strike. You are here today among the other groups of men because the Commander needs more teams of exceptional men for a second important mission. Several years ago he ordered a search for the brightest young men in Pakistan.

Soft Target
by Larry Greer

The twelve of you make up one of these important teams. In a little less than two years you will leave this camp to put your plan into action. Much of your time will be spent learning what Rallhas has introduced you to in the past four days. These will be the tools for your mission. Towards the end of your time here, you will learn the logistics of how to carry out your mission." So that none of us missed his final and most important point, the volume of Valdess' voice decreased to just above a whisper. We sat in total silence, almost fearing to breathe.

"You are now official members of Allah's Al-Qaida Army. In two years, the 'S' cell, which is the twelve of you, will be part of a second victory on the soil of the United States of America!!"

With that pronouncement, you could physically observe the chills that ran down Raga and Johey's backs. I was experiencing some of those same chills, but I managed to sit rigidly still and never batted an eye. My jaw locked, as if I knew that this would mean martyrdom for the twelve of us. To serve Allah in this very important mission, gave me the understanding that I now knew my spiritual destiny. All the way from my small village in Jiba I could feel my father's pride. As the information sunk in, it suddenly became clear to me, as it must have to the others that we would never again go home. Pride, anticipation and sadness wove through my heart. From now on, we twelve were one. We had just been entrusted with a great secret in the Al-Qaida army.

CHAPTER 7

Commonwealth of Virginia, United States of America

John Massey thought of himself as just a county boy. He had grown up just west of Ashville, North Carolina in the Smokey Mountains on a small farm his family had owned dating back to the Civil War. At an early age, John realized that following in his father's footsteps as a farmer, held no appeal. So he selected a course of study in college that would qualify him for foreign intelligence work. He was fortunate to be picked up for entry level work at the CIA immediately out of college. John was tall and lean with thick brown hair that glinted red in the light, and he sported abundant freckles that draped across his nose. When he added his broad friendly smile, you would not think "CIA" when you looked at him. Friends told him he looked out of place in the "CIA uniform" of stark black suit and tie. It did not take long for the nickname of 'Country Boy' to be widely touted. By this time, John had served over twenty-two years with 'the company' as the CIA was called, and had attained a senior ranking. Although he was not aggressively ambitious, he was proud of his accomplishments with "the company" and felt certain there were yet more opportunities available to him.

After the United States was attacked on September 11, 2001, the world, for John, would never be the same. His area of responsibility included intelligence gathering. Unfortunately, the new laws put in place after the attack, severely complicated his efforts. He often found himself frustrated with these constraints and he feared that his efforts were futile.

Soft Target
by Larry Greer

Today, as he drove through the foothills of Virginia to his office in Langley, his thoughts were on his son Jason, who was a sophomore in college. John and his wife were very proud of their son's accomplishments. Jason was not only a scholar, but an athlete. He was attending Hartwell University in South Carolina on full scholarship as a kicker on their highly rated ACC football team. As they had done when Jason was on the high school team, they attended every game. John's friends were all avid college football fans and told him frequently that Jason could make a big difference in the extra point category. He had been red shirted for his freshman year, and John was fine with that. He wanted Jason to get on solid academic footing before focusing on football.

As John neared his office, he entered a shopping center, and noticed that Macy's was having a sale. He must remember to pick up Molly's birthday gift during his lunch hour. He pulled into the parking garage. To the casual passer-by, this garage looked to be part of that shopping center. It was constructed for the express purpose of providing additional security and secrecy for this CIA office. He entered the Mall through the revolving doors walked down the corridor of small shops and eateries. He stopped at Starbucks to get his usual cup of "joe" and then continued through the Mall to a partly hidden door off the main concourse that said 'Authorized Employees Only.' He pressed his thumb to the pad, and the door clicked. He entered and as he always did, glanced over his shoulder to ensure no one would tailgate him as he entered. The entrance was programmed to verify that the person who had pressed their thumb print on the security pad was the same one entering and the only one entering. This high-tech security accounted for height and weight as well as cornea impressions. Once verified, John stepped onto the elevator. As a final verification, a sophisticated camera compared facial features to his CIA security files. John's office was actually a bomb-proof bunker, six stories underground. Once the shopping center had

Soft Target
by Larry Greer

been completed, it allowed for completely secure and private construction of an underground elevator to be built. Baltic Construction Company, an arm of the CIA, dropped elevator shafts to connect with the intelligence-gathering offices six stories below. This bunker-style complex had been built years before and anyone affiliated with that construction was now long gone. Few people even in the government knew about this big concrete bunker nestled deep underground. John exited the elevator and walked down the hall to his office, greeting the third shift as they wrapped up their work and prepared to head home. He stepped into the night shift supervisor's office.

"How's it going Charley?"
"John, did you see the news last night?"
"No. Molly and I went to a friend's for dinner. What's up?"

Silence! Charley was obviously stressed by this news. For several seconds he struggled searching for the right words. Then suddenly he just blurted it out,
"Those Dam Yellow-Crats in Congress are trying to fuck up our homeland security." Charley had long been vocal in his political conservatism and loved calling the opposing party "yellow-crats". "Did you know they are telling the President that he has to stop "eavesdropping" unless we have permission from the FISA Court? Those damn judges in the Foreign Intelligence Surveillance Court don't give a fuck about this country. For all they care, the Arabs can walk right in the front door and fight us on our own soil. They probably think that would be a benefit so our soldiers wouldn't have to leave our shores to fight. It's all about them getting the fuckin' votes and illegal power." Charley continued without even taking a breath. His face began to redden and John was sure his blood pressure was rising to a dangerous level as it always did when he got riled up. "You know what this all means? Well, I'll tell you what it fuckin' means…It means that when we pick up an

Soft Target
by Larry Greer

incoming call from Afghanistan or anywhere else in the damn world, for that matter, we have to get a lawyer on the phone. Then they have to wake up a FISA Court judge, who's supposed to be on call. And if we're lucky and he's not screwing his secretary or shit-faced drunk, we just might get his permission to let us do our damn job."

Although John was dismayed by this news, he decided that it would be best to let Charley complete his rant without interruption, and then he might be able to calm him enough to get rational details.

Charley continued his agitated words, "by the time all <u>that</u> takes place our caller will have dropped off the line, and we got nothing'. I mean absolutely, friggin' nothing'!"
This was not a total surprise to John. He had heard rumors to this effect several months ago, but had heard nothing recently.

"Well, Charley that will really tie our hands and a lot of calls will get through once the terrorist hear about this. In fact, I'll bet they have already picked it up on CNN or Fox. This is very disturbing, Charley. I can see how upset you are. Go home and get some sleep and call me when you wake up."

John's group of intelligence gatherers, were known as "The Call Center". This bomb-proof bunker was self-sustaining. In case of emergency, John's team could survive for 2 months without replenishment. At the center of the common area room were two heavy steel square tubes, large enough for two men at a time to enter. Ladders hung from two opposite sides stretching up the six stories to ground level. In case of emergency, elevators were cordoned off and all personnel were to ascend by way of the tubes. At several points on the ascent were landings, equipped with metal and concrete cutting saws should the need arise to cut away debris. John was mulling the situation, as he sipped his coffee. His Call Center had a good rapport with the Pentagon. Timely information from his men had averted at least a dozen terrorist threats since *Nine-Eleven*. This new directive would definitely prevent his men from keeping the Pentagon effectively informed of imminent or even potential danger. Charley was right. This new direction from Washington was dangerous for homeland security. The "Yellow-Crats" as Charley called them were using this in a raw grab for power in this election-year politics. Although John understood Charley's concerns, he didn't concur with Charley about the certainty of the outcome. John felt that if nothing else, the Supreme Court would weight in on this matter and someone would come to their senses. However, timing of the political wheels was a concern. He knew he would not have to wait long for new orders to make their way to his in-box. It was going to be tough to ask his staff to sit by and do nothing, while suspected terrorists made their coded calls. The opposing party was claiming that Americans' constitutional rights were being abused when their phones were monitored. In John's educated opinion, if a known terrorist was calling an American, it was not to talk about weather in Bagdad! John prided himself as a very rational, experienced CIA professional. But, this made his blood boil. As he sat there pondering what all this meant to the important work of his team, the phone rang. The voice on the other end of the line said,

"The 'big potato' is on the line for you. It was an affectionate nickname for John's boss, Milton West. Milton's shape had long been similar to a rotund russet potato.

"John, this is Milt."

"Good morning Sir."

"John, I suppose you have already heard the news about FISA, right?"

Soft Target
by Larry Greer

"Yes sir and I can tell you that it truly disturbs me. How in the hell are we going to operate effectively now?"

"Well, for the time being the President has the power to extend our eavesdropping for at least several more weeks. In the meantime, those of us in the intelligence community are going to fight it with all we've got. I'll know more when I get specifics from the Attorney General."

John hung up and wondered what would happen to his people and their work. He had three shifts of twelve. By government standards, that was a small department. But they were specially trained experts and with the help of a few carefully selected, outside telecommunications sub-contractors, had proven their worth to the country repeatedly. He worried about their future. In this underground command center, he had responsibility for almost twelve thousand square feet. It included state-of-the-art listening devices, plus sleeping quarters, food and survival equipment if needed. This small group monitored millions of cell phones and text messages plus internet communications. John knew that if the CIA and Homeland Security could successfully fight this eavesdropping ban, the country would stand a chance against al-Qaeda. In John's opinion, proponents of this bill (Charley's "yellow-crats") were not looking out for Americans. They just wanted the President to look bad and wanted the next Presidential election at any cost. John agreed with one of Charley's concerns; the "yellow-crats" just did not give a damn. He worried that this small group of politicians, hated the President so much that they were not acting rationally. He worried that this action would unintentionally benefit the enemy. He and Charley had discussed politics frequently over drinks after work. Charley told him frequently that the current slate of "yellow-crat" candidates was incompetent, inexperienced politicians. He often told John that if General Motors, was looking for a new CEO, "these politicians would not even make it into the top 100". Given this recent eavesdropping recommendation, even John wondered that if the opposition party were to get into office, were they competent to run and protect the most powerful country in the world.

John Massey left that day with a heavy heart and lot on his mind. However, even with all this going on, John did not forget Molly's birthday. There was a surprise party for her that night and he had something special in mind.

CHAPTER 8

The Announcement

The "S" cell team was now in their 18th month of training. It had been long and agonizing. The young men were now approaching eighteen and were homesick for their families and villages. There had been no contact with the outside world except for a few newspapers that made their way into camp. After almost 2 years in camp, they knew their lives were committed to Allah. Going back home to their old lives and friends would never happen. Mohamed did not yet know specifically what their mission was, but he suspected it was going to have world-wide significance and they would live up to their name 'Special Team'.

While assembled in the assigned training space for the "S" team, Valdess called out to Mohamed and ask him to come directly to his office. Raga and Johey looked at Mohamed fearing that he might have done something wrong. Because they were the newest recruits among many soldiers, they did not know that Valdess even knew their names. After their morning training, Mohamed quickly made his to way Valdess' office, and stood silently waiting to be recognized. Mohamed sat as directed on the only other chair in the room. It gave him a strange feeling to sit in a chair, as the standard seat was a spot on the ground or a carpet. Not only was this the only unoccupied chair in Valdese's office, it was only one of two chairs in the entire camp. Valdess appeared to ignore Mohamed as he concentrated on the stack of papers on his desk. After what

Soft Target
by Larry Greer

seemed like hours, Valdess slowly raised his head and looked up at Mohamed.

"My apologies Mohamed, but I needed to carefully review the instructions sent from the Commander before you and I could speak."

Reference to the Commander put a chill up Mohamed's back. This "Commander" had never appeared in person at the camp, but was mentioned with reverence by the senior officers. Mohamed thought of him as a mythical character.
No name had ever been attached to him other than "Commander".

"Mohamed," Valdess paused, for a moment, scratching his beard, as if pondering his next few words.

"We have carefully observed and evaluated the 12 of you in the "S" Team for the past 18 months. There are numerous areas that are important to your mission. Fitness, leadership and obedience to Allah are critical to your success. As with any mission, this one needs a strong leader. As you trained, we studied you all carefully to identify the most qualified among you for this task. I know you have been curious about specifics of the mission. It will be revealed soon, as your mission is at hand. Once the purpose of your mission is revealed to the "S" Team, there will be no turning back. Part of our decision is that we will use all 12 of you on the mission. As a group, you performed up to our expectations. You were all selected for your quickness, your intelligence and your dedication to Allah. You, Mohamed, have performed above our expectations and beginning tomorrow, you will assume leadership of the team. I am telling you this now, as tomorrow we will receive a very special visitor. He will meet with leaders of this entire camp and you will be among that group."

Soft Target
by Larry Greer

Mohamed thought to himself, "I cannot believe this. I cannot grasp what this means. I think I am feeling sick to my stomach, and I am sure that my face must look pale." Valdess noticed Mohamed's rare display of emotion and asked if he was OK.

Mohamed responded, "Yes Sir, I did not expect this honor. But, I will not disappoint you, the Commander or others who trusted me with this responsibility. I praise Allah for this opportunity and assure you that I will not fail this important mission."

Valdess responded, "Mohamed, I know you will not fail or we would not have selected you. You have grown into a fine man and have accomplished much since you enrolled into the Madrassas over five years ago. Your father would be proud of you. I might as well tell you now, that our special visitor is the Commander. As I said, you will be among the leaders of the camp and will be introduced as the chosen leader of the 'S' cell. The Commander will not be surprised, as he has been kept informed about our observations of the "S" Cell team. He will be pleased."

As was his style, Valdess paused, then continued,

"After mid-day prayers tomorrow, as we all gather to eat our noon meal, I will announce our decision to all in the camp. Unless you have any questions, you may leave. Rejoin your team, but under no conditions do you say anything about this conversation. All will be revealed soon."

As I rose to leave, I turned back, "Thank you, Sir." It was all I could think to say. I felt light headed as I walked across the large expanse of the covered shelter. I thought to myself, "Am I capable of this leadership? Is their faith in my ability misplaced? Once I joined my team, the daily exercises and training removed my queasiness and focused on the running, climbing and calisthenics. Because of the conversation with Valdess, today's fitness training took on a new meaning for me. We were close.

Soft Target
by Larry Greer

Although I still did not know what our mission was, I knew preparation was critical. I was proud of the results of all my physical training. I was much stronger, both physically and mentally than when I arrived. Raga and Johey made a point to position themselves next to me. They immediately began to grill me about why Valdess wanted to talk to me. What did he say? Did I know the purpose of our mission? On and on they questioned. For the first time in a long time, I allowed myself to grin and teased them. This evasive response frustrated Raga and Johey, but our routine did not allow them any more time for questioning. After the mid-day prayer when everyone was assembled and ready for our noon meal, Valdess stepped onto the platform and cleared his throat,

"Men, I need your attention." The gathering was instantly silent.

"This is a very important announcement. As you all know, the 'S' cell is one of the very important teams at this camp. You all will soon be part of a very important mission. Today we will focus on the 'S' cell's accomplishments. Their training is almost complete and their mission will commence in the next few months. We have observed these twelve men carefully for nearly 2 years. It is now time to reveal who will lead this team."

Mohamed could feel the heat rise from his neck up his face and was certain that the blush on his cheeks would reveal the announcement before Valdess could speak the words. He thought he felt Johey and Raga cutting their eyes toward him. Valdess continued.

"Today, I am pleased to announce that Mohamed of Jiba has been chosen to lead the 'S'cell."

Soft Target
by Larry Greer

The silence that ensued felt like it continued for an eternity, but suddenly the one hundred soldiers across the camp let out loud shouts of approval.

After our mid-day prayers and meal, as was the custom, we headed to our bunks for some much cherished rest. A short 30 minutes later our afternoon classes would begin. Raga, Johey and I had always bunked together. And I was not surprised when Raga peered down over the edge of his top bunk and grinned at me.

"I suppose now Johey and I will have to address you as "Sir"?"

Because I was not yet used to this new leadership position, I did not immediately know how to respond. So, I just let out a small laugh and teased,

"That's right, and now is a good time for you to start."

Both Raga and Johey groaned. However, they knew things would never be the same between the three of them, so they acquiesced and gave Mohamed his first "Yes, Sir."

Soft Target
by Larry Greer

CHAPTER 9

The Commander

The morning after my leadership position had been announced, we gathered as usual, in the square. We were told to get into formation, remain silent and stand at attention. Valdess announced,

"This morning we have an important visitor. The air was electric with anticipation, but absolute silence remained, as an imposing man emerged out of one of the doorways. Two soldiers appeared behind him toting automatic weapons. He was tall, with a long gray beard, a white robe and turban. He paused, leaning on a knotted staff and surveyed the crowd. He spoke quietly to Valdess for a moment and then stepped onto the riser. When he spoke, it was not in Arabic or English or even Spanish as the soldiers had been practicing. Instead his words were in Urdu, the Pakistani national language. We were surprised and impressed.

Every man in camp figured out that this was the elusive "Commander". No one except Valdess and Rallhas had ever seen his face.

Raga leaned to me and asked,

"Is that who I think it is?" I did not respond but continued to look straight ahead.

Soft Target
by Larry Greer

I was nervous, given my new position and wanted to make sure I made a good impression on our Commander, Osama bin Laden. He surveyed the soldiers, all of us still standing at attention. He turned and made another quiet comment to Valdess. Slowly turning again to the soldiers, he began to speak.

"My fellow soldiers, Allah has selected you for an important mission. You have been trained for the purpose of serving your country and protecting our ways of life from threats of the Western infidels. I have been kept informed of your progress and am pleased. You are the cream of our mother's milk and your work will save your beloved country Pakistan for our children and our children's children. This is a momentous day. Today we are all part of al-Qaeda, the army of Allah. Today you are no longer a student. Now you join me as a soldier for Allah. From this day forward, you will spend time with your leaders and strategists planning your missions. When our plans are revealed to the world, the infidels will be shocked by our dedication to this jihad. Allah does not instruct us to turn the other cheek as the infidel's God recommends. We are now prepared to fight." The students, newly named as part of the al-Qaeda army, responded to bin Laden: "Praise to Allah". Bin Laden continued.

"The attacks on American soil on September, 11, 2001 were only the beginning of our jihad. The infidels believe that they have stopped us, but they are wrong. Their minds have become clouded and corrupted with greed. Even now, they relax their airport security and handcuff their intelligence agencies. Unlike our al-Qaeda soldiers, they are not focused on protecting their own country. Their politicians spend all their time fighting with each other and are unwittingly helping our cause. Their soldiers cannot win on our soil and are not prepared to fight us on their own land." There were heads nodding in agreement and murmurs of ascent from the soldiers. Osama bin Laden persisted over the murmurs,

Soft Target
by Larry Greer

"You have been formed into many small teams of insurgents at this training camp. And this camp is only one of many with many teams such as yours. In the near future, your mission will be to take our jihad to the enemy's home turf. Praise Allah." With that, bin Laden raised his hand in salute to his new soldiers and stepped back into Valdese's office. As the soldiers began to disperse, Rallhas approached me and directed me to report to Valdess' office. I knew that bin Laden had gone into the office and assumed this was the meeting that Valdess had referenced yesterday. As I approached Valdese's office I noted the armed guards flanking the door. Valdess motioned for me to enter. Several leaders were standing, talking quietly in small groups. Bin Laden was sitting on a pillow near the back of the room. He motioned for Valdess and several others, including myself, to join him. My stomach clenched and my mouth felt parched. I selected a spot on the floor next to, and a little behind Valdess. It gave me a good view of bin Laden, but also some little distance, so I could observe.

Bin Laden's face appeared tired and wrinkles encircled his eyes and lined his forehead. He appeared older than the photographs I had seen of him. He must be under immense pressure. Perhaps he had been ill. Commander bin Laden was the first to speak. I was shocked and surprised as he directed his comments solely to me.

"I would like to congratulate you Mohamed for being the chosen one to lead one of our most important missions. Your mission will be the first of many we have planned for America. Thus, it is very important to our success. Do you understand?" I managed a nod of comprehension.

"Our intelligence tells us that the infidels believe we could never successfully attack them again. We have kept them guessing. Their Homeland Security takes credit for what they call

Soft Target
by Larry Greer

our failure to carry out more attacks. We know that is not true. The truth is that we learned a great deal on September 11 and have been preparing ourselves for the next successful jihad attack. That time is now. This mission will be complete next year in 2008. Our target will again be the United States of America. The location cannot be revealed to you or your men until after you have set foot on infidel soil. This is for your security and that of your men. There are already members of our army in America ready to assist you with logistics of your mission. You will be given phone numbers and e-mail addresses to contact them as necessary. One of our most trusted operatives is an American citizen who will be your primary contact. He will help guide and assist in anyway you see fit. You will leave Pakistan and head to Mexico. You will cross the Mexican-American border in April of 2008. From there you will work your way to the target area with the help of operatives called "Mexican Coyotes". You will be provided with official-looking documents that will enable you to secure legitimate jobs at the target location prior to your strike. The English and Spanish languages you have learned will be critical to your success. Beginning tomorrow Mohamed, you and your team will spend all your time studying the logistics of your mission. You will first be traveling to Islamabad and then fly to Venezuela in South America. From there you will head to Mexico and then on to the United States of America. Three highly-trained men will join us here in the camp in a few days. They will familiarize you with traveling in America. From them you will learn how to read road maps and necessary geography of the target area for your mission. You will also be taught American customs and culture. Learning how to act American will allow you to blend in. Success of your mission will depend on not drawing attention to yourselves as Arabs. That is enough detail for today. Mohamed, I may see you and your teams before you leave, but if not, I wish you success and may Allah be with you." With that bin Laden stood up, gripped my arm, and bid me goodbye. I was never to see him again.

Soft Target
by Larry Greer

CHAPTER 10

Vatican City – Rome

Carlos Mendias was growing weary of his job. He had worked in the Vatican maintence department for twelve years. Although he knew he should feel honored to work at the Vatican, he could not adopt the Catholic dogma. His religion was different. He was within 60 days of turning thirty. Although he made good money, it was still not enough to support his family. His heritage frowned on women working and so, although it was against Vatican policy, he drove a cab on the weekend to make the necessary extra cash for his children's private school. He wanted more meaning in his job and his life. When he was only 18, a brother from his homeland had approached him about serving his god in a different way. As a result of that meeting, he had decided to join the brotherhood. This arrangement meant that he would have to lead a double life by keeping his Muslim heritage a secret. Not only did he have to keep his membership in the brotherhood a secret, but it meant he had to change his name. Carlos Mendias was the name he had selected when applying for work at the Vatican. He had been born *Abdul Azeez*. In his homeland of Pakistan, his name meant, "servant of the most powerful." Joining the brotherhood made him feel there would come a time when he would live up to that name. As a boy, he had studied at the Madrassa School and memorized the entire Quran. This accomplishment bestowed on him the privilege of being termed a

Soft Target
by Larry Greer

hafiz. He could now be called *Hafiz Abdul Azeez*. It also gave him status in the brotherhood. This group was in reality a sleeper cell operating in Rome for al-Qaeda. To further his commitment to al-Qaeda, Carlos married a local Catholic girl and they now had two children. Maintaining this double life was a strain that few could have endured. He was so good at the deception, attending Mass every Sunday and sending his children to private Catholic school, that his wife had no inkling of his secret life.

His dedication to al-Qaeda required that he gain the confidence of his employer. He did this so successfully that, even as a young man, he advanced quickly to shop foreman. All of the Vatican cars, trucks and other vehicles came to his shop for repairs. The famous "Pope Mobile" was included in the fleet that came under Carlos's supervision and care.

It was Carlos's habit, to eat his lunch his wife prepared for him, out in his pickup. He liked the respite from the other mechanics. He liked to listen to the radio and most of all, within that truck; he could leave the pretense of being Carlos and truly be *Hafiz Abdul Azeez*. Today, he anxiously opened his truck door. It was an old American GMC pick-up truck, battered with over a hundred-thousand miles on its speedometer. He always left it unlocked because here on Vatican property, behind the guarded fence, he felt safe. As he opened the heavy driver door, the large brown envelope he had anticipated, fell from the truck onto the ground. He noticed there was no name on the envelope. Because it had fallen out of his truck, he felt comfortable opening the sealed envelope. Inside, he found yet another sealed envelope. It was closed with a familiar red wax seal. With nervous fingers, he opened the smaller envelope. On a piece of non-descript white paper, the writing began: As your name indicates, you are a faithful servant to Allah. The brotherhood is now calling on you to serve with your brothers. You will play an important role in a critical mission for al-Qaeda. For your safety, your name will not

Soft Target
by Larry Greer

be used on any documents, and for security of the mission, you will be given information only about your part of the jihad. Your ID is now "S 13". Any future communication will be delivered as this envelop was. We have acquired a key to your truck so that we can deliver and retrieve messages. We will now require you to lock the door of your truck.

    Here is what we require of you. On April15th, of this year the Pope will visit America. His first destination is Washington DC. From there he will fly to New York City. His itinerary indicates that he will be on American soil for approximately six days before returning to the Vatican. He will be taking his Pope Mobile on this trip. Your task is to hide twelve automatic pistols somewhere inside that vehicle. The pistols will be retrieved when he lands in America by others in the brotherhood. American customs officers will not closely check the Pope's personal equipment, assuming his private security will have done that. Your first task will be to devise a plan and leave the details in an unmarked envelope on the seat of your truck. You will do this by February 1st. Memorize, as we know you can do, the key parts to this memo, and then burn it. 'S 13', the Commander and the brotherhood are counting on you. This last comment gave Carlos, alias, Hafiz Abdul Azeez, a feeling of pride.

    This was just the meaning Carlos wanted in his life. Over the next few weeks, he spent every spare moment he could find in private to devise a plan to hide the pistols in the Pope Mobile. After completing the report, he read it three times to ensure he had left nothing to chance. He placed the report in a white envelope, sealed it with red wax and deposited that envelope in a large manila folder on his driver's seat on February 1st as directed.

    Carlos's plan read as follows: The Pope Mobile is small, but it is designed to be bullet-proof and made of heavy steel. It weighs exactly 8,228 pounds. The pistols weight 5.2 pounds each

Soft Target
by Larry Greer

or 62.4 pounds for the twelve. I will make an opening underneath the seat, in the bottom of the vehicle. I will remove 66 pounds of support metal. I will add supports to secure the pistols in place. These supports will weigh 3.6 lbs. If by chance, the vehicle is weighed going through American Customs, the weight will not arouse suspicions. I am also purchasing a stainless finished tool box for my truck. It will have the capability of being locked. It will fit in the bed of my truck. It will not seem unusual for a mechanic to have a tool box and to avoid suspicion it will always contain some tools. I will brag about the purchase and show it off to the security guards at the gate. Then as I pass through the gate day after day they will not think to check the contents. At the appropriate time you will place the pistols in my truck under a false bottom I have created. Each gun should be packed in a heat resistance bag. The compartment in the Pope Mobile is near the exhaust pipe. The bags will prevent damage to the guns.
Please confirm that my preparations are acceptable to the brotherhood. Praise Allah.

Soft Target
by Larry Greer

CHAPTER 11

Islamabad, Pakistan

Valdess knew that this mission must be flawless, so he took personal charge of the logistics that would transport the team every step of the way from the mountain training camp to America. After that, it would be totally in Mohamed's hands.
Valdess had already completed the first contact with 'S 13' in Rome. He was now awaiting the appointed time to review and evaluate 'S13's plan. The next "S" cell member he needed to contact would serve as a travel agent. He decided this needed to be done in person. This operative would be called 'S14'. He would develop the master plan for the long journey from Northern Pakistan to America. This piece of the mission was extremely critical. There could be no mistakes. The initial twelve 'S' team members must travel in complete anonymity. No part of their travels could call attention to these al Qaeda soldiers. Therefore, he needed the most qualified person to handle this job.

The cell member's name was Larkawa Khas. He was twenty-eight years old and eager to be part of this jihad. His appearance gave him the aura of an intellectual book-worm. He wore thick coke-bottle eyeglasses. His hair was frequently disheveled and his clothes were always rumpled. He worked in logistics for a local manufacturer, but also secretly operated as an informant for the Pakistani Intelligence Agency. He had a passion for al Qaeda and had applied to join the insurgency and fight in

Soft Target
by Larry Greer

Iraq. Although disappointed when he was turned down, he maintained his fervor for the cause. What he didn't know was that he had been turned down as a soldier because the al Qaeda leaders had him in mind for a more important assignment. Larkawa was half Pakistani and half Indian. He spoke four languages, including English and Spanish, and six dialects. Valdess felt he was perfect for this mission.

Valdess would have to travel from the mountain camp south to Taxila then to Islamabad, a six-hundred mile journey. Because this mission was so critical, Valdess was uncomfortable traveling great distances by himself, so he hired a driver and several guards. They were dressed as civilians, but were well armed with pistols and grenades hidden beneath their clothing. The roads traveling through Pakistan south to Islamabad were rural and frequently were fraught with roadside bandits. If anyone appeared to want them to stop, they would speed up and lift their pistols in the air as a warning. It was now the rainy season in Pakistan, and the roads were like muddy washboards. The government invested very little money improving the infrastructure of Pakistan, instead spending it on the military. The government feared India and its emerging international status and military power. Although the Pakistani government was well aware of al-Qaeda and its mission, it did not recognize the jihad publically. When persistent Western forces insisted al Qaeda was operating along their northern border of Afghanistan, the Pakistani government vehemently denied any connection.

In the minds of many Pakistanis, following a military coup of 1999, Pervez Musharraf, became the unofficial president of Pakistan. Musharraf was wary of al-Qaeda and took great care to avoid any direct conflict with them. Musharraf's avoidance tactics worked in al-Qaeda's favor, making it easy to crisscross the northern border between Pakistan and Afghanistan and elude US troops who only operated in Afghanistan.

Soft Target
by Larry Greer

Upon arriving in Islamabad, Valdess connected with Larkawa. They agreed to meet the next morning at a sidewalk coffee shop. This public meeting place would not arouse suspicion....just two friends enjoying coffee in the morning sun. Valdes's soldiers, still disguised as civilians, sat at a table close by and casually watched the crowd for anything unusual. Although Valdess and Larkawa had never met, as agreed, they displayed affection as if they had been childhood friends. Valdess initiated the discussion by giving Larkawa his 'S 14' title. As Valdess had done with "S 13", he explained that this was for his protection and for the security of their mission. Very little information would be written down on paper. If he did receive written communication, it was to be committed to memory and immediately burned. Absolutely nothing was to be communicated via computer, as they all knew that any information on hard drives could be recovered by the enemy.

Valdess instructed, "You will have one of the most important parts to play in our mission. I cannot stress strongly enough that you must be extremely careful in all you do from now on. The weight of the mission's success is now on your shoulders. There cannot be any blunders. Do you understand?" Larkawa nodded solemnly.

"A team of twelve men will be traveling from Taxila down to Islamabad on January 1st. When they arrive in Islamabad, you will arrange a place to meet and communicate your plans for this trip. You and I will not meet again, as I am known by many in this part of Pakistan and it would be dangerous. At the foot of my chair is a small package for you to pick up as you leave the café. It contains an untraceable cellphone. We will communicate from now in this way. I will call you precisely two weeks from today. You will inform me where the 'S' cell will be sequestered for a couple of days before beginning the second leg of their journey. I will be the only one calling you on this phone. Names will not be necessary. If you must make reference to the leader of this group, he is to be referred to as "S1". Once you have planned the remaining legs of their journey and they have departed Islamabad, you will have no more direct contact with them. I will be 'S'1's only contact throughout the remainder of the mission. The last communication you have with me will be to leave me with the travel plans you have made for the "S Cell". One very important point, Larkawa, currently "S 1" believes that when his team leaves Venezuela, they will travel through Mexico to America. You must make plans to take them directly from Venezuela to America. This miss-information was purposefully left with "S 1", to protect the team in case someone compromises our plan."

    Larkawa now understood the importance of his role in this jihad. Getting the "S Cell" safely through each of the legs of their trip was most critical. Although he felt a great weight of responsibility, he was not daunted by the task. His work both in logistics and as an informant for the government in Islamabad, gave him important connections at many levels.

CHAPTER 12

Rome, Italy

On February 1st, as instructed, Carlos Mendias left a detailed description of his part of the mission in a brown envelope on the seat of his truck that sat in the Vatican compound. When he came back to the truck after work that evening, the envelope was gone. Carlos was both excited and fearful. He had put himself at great risk, checking the Pope Mobile to ensure he could create a secret compartment for the pistols. He put the vehicle on a lift. If he had been interrupted making this inspection, it would look as if he was preparing to change the oil. As Carlos inspected the vehicle, he realized that he had forgotten about the location of the spare tire. This made his plan even easier. The spare tire was secured in a hinged compartment directly under the seat. When he felt certain that he was alone, he dropped the heavy lid. Secured to the lid was an fullsize spare tire. Carlos quickly measured the compartment that held the tire. By removing the tire, it created a perfect space for the pistols. He would not even have to make alterations to the vehicle. His biggest fear had been how he would cut the metal to create the space for the pistols. He would have had to use a cutting torch and that would have been extremely risky. Now he simply needed to remove the spare tire, and carefully duct tape the bags which contained the pistols, to the lid, close it and lock it. This was almost too easy.

Four days later, Carlos's plan had made it to Valdess in Taxila, Pakistan. Valdess was extremely pleased with Carlos's

Soft Target
by Larry Greer

work. He had devised a perfect hiding place for the pistols in the Pope Mobile. Valdess read this with a smile on his face and immediately burned the correspondence.

CHAPTER 13

Caracas, Venezuela

"Miguel." Mondo's loud voice came from some distance and reverberated down the long tube. "Yaaa?" came the response from Miguel.

"Do you not get claustrophobic in this thing?"
"Nooo," said Miguel. --- Mondo responded,
"Well, you will never catch me down under with the hatch closed."
Miguel retorted with a laugh,
"Well if you were in this tub and the hatch was NOT closed, you would be one dead Sweally"(This was Miguel's slang for a Venezuelan).

This "boat" was unique and had been a special project of Hugo Chavez, President of Venezuela. He had long been fascinated with the U-boats built by Hitler during WWII. The boat design that Miguel and Mondo were now working on was a scaled-down version of one of Hitler's U-boats, with much updated equipment. Chavez was spending huge amounts of his oil revenues on weapons and creation of a small, well-equipped Navy. This boat had been designed by highly-skilled Russian submarine engineers. The most important feature of this U-boat was the silent nature of its engines. It emitted no sound and was virtually undetectable by the sophisticated US subs, even with their state-of-the-art sonar equipment. This mini-sub had been named the "UV", for "Undetectable Vehicle". Miguel and Mondo were making final inspections and tests, to ensure it was fully ready for its next mission. The boat was 108 feet in length with a 14-foot beam was 10 feet in height. It had the capacity for carrying 18 men. It could remain submerged for four weeks without surfacing for supplies. Its power source came from breakthrough lithium battery technology provided by Russian scientists. It had 182 tiny dynamos, no larger than a man's fist. These dynamos were implanted into the outer skin of the sub. As the boat moved through the water, the force from the water turned the small fans like water wheels on their sides. This process kept the big batteries constantly charged while the sub was in motion. The boat was also equipped with a state-of-the-art satellite navigation system, designed to tap into the satellite signals of freighters, tankers or even nearby nuclear submarines, directly above the UV, without detection. This technology allowed the sub to travel like a parasite, twenty to thirty feet below, yet electronically attached to the ship above. Its maximum speed was twenty one knots, which would allow it to maintain the same speed as most fully loaded ships. When entering ports, the UV would come closer to the surface, but remain out of sight. Its strategy was to surface at night time and dock quickly at an unoccupied slip. It would remain only long enough for the "S Cell" to disembark, then quickly submerge and relocate its self until the mission was complete. A four-man crew could operate it in four six hour shifts.

    Miguel belonged to the brotherhood. During a recent meeting of al-Qaeda brothers, Miguel had been selected to serve in an important capacity. He was to be the captain of the UV and had been given extremely secretive orders for this mission. He was now aware of the twelve "S team" members currently making their way to Venezuela. Now, Captain Miguel was to prepare the UV boat with five days of provisions for sixteen men. He was one of the few privy to the destination of the journey. He knew they would be traveling two thousand miles directly to America. They were to depart on February 12th and had been instructed to electronically "attach themselves" to the Brazilian freighter 'Zoe

Two'. This freighter fit their mission perfectly, as the Zoe Two would cross the Gulf of Mexico into New Orleans.

    Miguel said nothing of this to Mondo who was only on board as a mechanic to make some adjustments on the drive shaft. Although Mondo was also a member of the brotherhood, he was not a part of this mission. He knew better than to ask questions about undertakings of the UV.

CHAPTER 14

South Carolina

The Board of Regents at Hartwell University in early 2007 decided to move forward with plans to enlarge the stadium by adding a west-end wing. The cost would be over sixty-five million dollars. With recent successes of the football team, this money would not be hard to generate. Those additional seats would also not be hard to fill and so the board felt that the ROI would be rather quick. The Hartwell University Stadium would now be one of the largest in the Southeast, holding over 80,000 fans. The first floor would house a workout room, a team meeting room and some very well-appointed locker rooms. The top floor would add six more private corporate boxes to the current complement of 32 and include high-end food service for its executive guests. This was to be a beautiful addition to the stadium. Hartwell Stadium was well known among fans and broadcasters. However, due to the unusual acoustics, visiting teams detested playing in this stadium. Because of the stadium design, crowd noise reverberated to create a decibel level that made it impossible to hear plays called. Pre-game festivities were also well known at Hartwell Stadium. It was tradition for Hartwell players to charge from the buses, down the hill and out onto the field. Adding to crowd excitement were the usual cannon explosions, followed by a very loud, very enthusiastic marching band. It was worth the price of a ticket to be there and witness these pre-game festivities. Now there would be 3,000 more voices in the west end joining this mayhem.

Soft Target
by Larry Greer

The most recent addition to the stadium were two mega-tron score boards, each 18 feet x 60 feet utilizing the latest technology, at each end of the field. An exciting addition for fans was its ability to instantly convert to live television for the purpose of highlighting other ESPN college games.

At the direction of Homeland Security, new guidelines had been developed by the government to handle situations of crowd violence and panic. It was now almost impossible to enter the stadium without being scrutinized by a security guard. Behind the scenes, a grid of Hot Lines had been set up that went directly to Home Land Security in Washington DC.

Larry Smith had been responsible for stadium logistics for over 15 years. He was now also responsible for construction of the new West End Zone. In February of 2008, Larry announced to the Board of Regents that construction was behind schedule. The goal had always been for the project to be complete in time for the big cross-state rivalry on November 29th. If it was going to happen, Larry admonished the Board that the general contractor would need authority to hire additional sub-contractors and they should expect cost over-runs. After a lengthy and heated debate, the Board of Regents begrudgingly agreed to his stipulation.

Soft Target
by Larry Greer

CHAPTER 15

The Journey Begins

My team had received word that we should make plans to leave the camp early in January. We would leave in three groups of four, much in the same way we had been brought into the camp. The second and third group would follow the first, each two days apart.

I set the expectation that they would depart, riding the same donkeys blind folded that had led us into the camp, almost 2 years earlier. We would travel back up through the mountains to a waiting van that would transport us to Taxila. There we would re-group and receive further orders. The entire trip back to Taxila would be conducted under the cover of darkness. As had been the case for the past few years, all this secrecy was for the purpose of concealing the location of our training camp.

After each of our three groups made the grueling trip to Taxila, we regrouped for the last time. It was now expected that we would never again be separated for the remainder of our mission. It was during this short layover in Taxila that Valdess met with me to go over logistics for the next portions of our trip to America.

"Mohamed, I have been working with an agent in Islamabad, now known to you as 'S'14. He has devised very detailed plans for your travels from Taxila to America. Your trip is to begin the day-after tomorrow. A truck will take your team from here to Islamabad. This journey will take several days. Each man will be outfitted with a combat rifle and a pistol. To avoid suspicion, you will travel in civilian clothes, which we will provide before you leave Taxila. An advance team from our camp will patrol the road so that insurgents, which have become very bothersome, will not attack your truck or impede your journey. These advance teams will be in constant contact with your driver. This is a taxing journey in a crowded truck so we have made arrangements after day-two, for you to spend time at a half-way house where you and your team can rest. At this point, you should expect 'S'14 to contact you and reveal the plan for the next three legs of your journey. You must commit the plans to memory for if you are caught in America with information regarding your mission; it could mean life in prison for all of you.

As promised, Valdess was at the departure point, two days later when the 'S' team loaded into the truck. Mohamed was last to board. As he turned to thank Valdes, he was surprised with an uncharacteristic embrace. These two men had become very close over the past two years. Valdess waved and wished them well as the truck began to roll.
"Allah be with you," he called out.

The trip to Islamabad was hot and dusty. The truck's wooden benches were unbearably cold and hard. Each pothole brought a jolt that made it impossible to find comfort or fall asleep. The men became unusually quiet, each lost in his own private thoughts. The first night they set up camp beside the truck, some finding soft spots to sleep in the grass and some preferring security beneath the truck. As the sun set on the second day, the truck left the main road, stopping at an old warehouse hidden behind a grove of trees. The soldiers, weary of their long, bumpy ride, climbed out and were greeted by four guards. They were escorted inside the warehouse and directed to where they would sleep for the next two nights. Facilities were sparse. Although there was running water, it was cold. After quickly washing up, they laid out their prayer

Soft Target
by Larry Greer

rugs, facing Mecca and said evening prayers. Following prayers, they shared a meal of dried dates, bread and cold meat, which had been laid out for them. Conversation was still minimal and they soon drifted toward their mats to sleep. Each one of them took a turn joining the four guards, on one-hour watches. Despite the added security, each man kept his weapons close by his side as he slept.

The next day-after morning prayers and their first meal, Mohamed said,

"Sometime today, we will meet a brother who will instruct us on the next part of our journey. You must pay very close attention to all he has to say. None of his instructions will be written down and you will not be allowed to make any notations."

CHAPTER 16

Pakistan to Caracas

A van drove up and stopped just short of two guards who were secluded within grove of trees where Mohamed and his men were resting. The man who got out of the van was tall. He wore dark sunglasses and a New York Yankee ball cap. His clothes did not look Pakistani, but more western. He nodded at the guards and indicated that he was here to speak with Mohamed. The guard proceeded to frisk him for weapons and finding none, pointed to where I was sitting, under a tree reading a foreign newspaper. Larkawa Khas greeted me saying,

"Buenos Dias Mohamed."

I looked up surprised that I had been addressed in Spanish. So I responded back in Spanish,

"Buenos Dias Senior."

Larkawa then reverted to English and reached out to shake Mohamed's hand.
"I am 'S14'. I assume you are expecting me."

I nodded, confirming that we had been expecting him.

"As you can see we are resting after our trip from the camp. Would you like to share a cup of tea with us before we get down to business?"

Soft Target
by Larry Greer

"Yes that would be pleasant here in the shade of the trees," said Larkawa. "We don't have many trees left in my city." He was careful to be vague about personal details.

Mohamed called out for one of the guards to bring tea and sent word to the others that they should join him and "S 14". After tea was served, I nodded for the guards to leave. They understood that something confidential was about to transpire and taking their rifles, they posted themselves along the road out of earshot.

After the team assembled under the tree, I introduced 'S'14 to them and said,
"I want you to listen very closely to what we are told about the next phase of our mission. "S 14" has prepared our journey.

Larkawa stood, cleared his voice and began.

"I am honored to be among such a chosen group of brothers. My small contribution to your important mission is logistics. Because I have contact with many members of the brotherhood, I can tell you that many are awaiting the day that they are called upon to do Allah's will. You are fortunate to have been selected. Your travels to America will mean great risk for each of you. As "S 1" indicated, you must pay very close attention. I will provide you with two sets of civilian clothes. Each of your clothes will be different from your brothers. Pay attention and notice differences in the shoes, shirts, pants and hats. The purpose of this difference is so that you cannot be identified as a group. Your goal is to blend in with the general population in Mexico. You will also notice that even your packs will look different. Some of you will receive tattered packs, and some will look like those a student might carry. Some of them have American university emblems on them. Pay attention to these and memorize the university they represent. Some of the shoes will look like average work boots, worn and old. Other shoes will be made of canvas which are called tennis shoes by Americans and are very common. Even your pants will differ in their appearance. This next instruction is very important. When you are ready to depart on the last leg of your journey, which will take you to America, you must discard the clothes you are now wearing and wear one of the packages of clothes I have put in your backpack. Does anyone have questions?" The group was silent so Larkawa continued.

"Tomorrow, you will embark on your long trip to Caracas, Venezuela. That will take you over eight thousand miles and across two continents. First, you will again load into the truck which brought you here. Your destination will be a small airport just outside the city. There you will board a small plane for your next leg. You will arrive in a city that is friendly to our brotherhood. Because of this, you will have no need for your weapons. Leave them on the truck. This plane will take you to Karachi, a city on our own Southern coast. Your pilots were extremely well trained in an American city called Fort Lauderdale, Florida. Like you, they are al-Qaeda. Larkawa smiled as he said this, but was not sure they understood the coincidence. (Larkawa was recalling the September 11 pilots who also trained at Fort Lauderdale.) Before you board the plane I will give each of you a sealed packet. In it will be 100 Bolivar, which is the Venezuelan currency. Additionally you will have a voucher for 10,000 additional Bolivars. After you land in Karachi, you will be taken to a small cruise ship owned by our revered leader, Osama bin Laden and his family. They are aware of your mission, but no one on the crew will ask questions and you will not discuss any details with any crew members. You will be treated as honored guests, so enjoy the two-day trip. As there will be others on board, you must mingle with the crowd. Look your best at all times and be polite, but quiet. Do not gather in your group of twelve. This boat trip will take 2 days. Your ship will land in Qatar at the Ad Dawhah port. You will be met and taken to a small hotel, operated by al-Qaeda. After a days rest, you will be picked up and transported to a private

Soft Target
by Larry Greer

executive airport. Here again, there will be no questions asked about your journey. In your pack, with your clothes, you will find an airline ticket with your name on it. At the private airport you will board a commercial airplane. After boarding you must find a way to destroy your ticket stub. There must be no trail of your travels. The next leg of your journey will take twelve hours. Most of you will be seated in economy class, but some in business class. Separating your seats like this is designed so you will not appear to be a group and arouse suspicion.

Upon arriving in Caracas, Venezuela, you will be met at the airport by a tour guide who will have a sign that reads 'BuenoS DiaS'. This sign will be spelled incorrectly, using two capital S's. You are traveling with only your backpacks, so no luggage will be checked. The guide will load you into a small bus and take you to your next destination is a port outside of Caracas, called Puerto Cabellos. This port is primarily used for large cruise ships and freighters. The ship you board will take you to Mexico. None of you will know which ship you are on until boarding time. This is for your own security.

The cash I mentioned earlier is for your personal needs such as food or toiletries. There is but one stipulation: any currency you have left before boarding the ship in Caracas should be given to the beggars on the street. Take nothing with you from Venezuela. There should be no trail that allows anyone to trace you back to South America. The vouchers I mentioned earlier are for your initial use in America. Your guide will convert these vouchers to American money that will equal $1,372 dollars. This exchange will occur before your board the boat. The American money is designed for your personal use during your first weeks in America.

Also in your packet is a map of Mexico, a list of cities and places in Mexico you should memorize. Once memorized, the list must be destroyed. There will also be a Green Card which lists your home address in Mexico. Your new Spanish names as well as that of your wife and children's names are included. You will tell anyone who asks that your family has remained in Mexico. All of this paperwork will establish your new identity. The documents will be very important if you get picked up by the immigration police. Keep them with you at all times once you reach the American shore. You are to speak Spanish and some broken English. We realize you actually speak excellent English but, it is not to your advantage to let others know this about you. Any contact with Americans must be avoided at this point or you could be mistaken for illegal Mexicans and be deported. My brothers, this is the extent of your journey. I have given you a great deal of information. Your leader will be responsible for additional details. If you have any questions, now is a good time to ask."

The members looked around at each other to see who would be the first to ask. Raga spoke up,

"We are twelve; will we always travel as twelve? We may attract attention traveling around as a group."

"That is an excellent question, responded Larkawa. "When you arrive in America, The cell member will explain how you are to travel and when it's safe to be together. Remember one thing; you must make every effort to assimilate as Mexicans in America. You speak their language and to the American infidels, you will look like Mexicans. The Mexicans of course will realize you are not Hispanic, but the less you say about your history, the easier they will accept you, especially since you are fluent in Spanish."

The meeting broke up after Larkawa cleared up a few more points. Mohamed went over to him and requested a private moment for additional questions. They walked around the building and after pausing for a moment he asked.

Soft Target
by Larry Greer

"I understand everything you have told us, up till now. What I want to know is, where in America will we end up and what is our ultimate target?"

Larkawa responded,

"Mohamed, I am sure you realize the complexity and great distance of this trip. As you already know, there are many brotherhood members who are facilitating your journey. None of them know more than the part in which they are involved. That is for our safety but primarily the security of your mission. What you are asking, I do not know myself. What happens when you arrive in America will be revealed by others along your journey. Only the Commander and Valdess know the complete plan. I am certain that in time they will communicate that to you." He nodded his head and departed.

CHAPTER 17

The New World Experience

    Because of Larkawa's careful planning, the team had traveled through Islamabad and arrived in Puerto Cabello, Venezuela without any problems. This coastal town was like a fairy-tale. Since most of us grew up in small rural villages, we had never experienced the luxury a city afforded. Spending hours lying in the sunshine around a pristine swimming pool had us enthralled. We were fascinated by the palm trees, the quantity and array of available foods and especially coconuts, (a food we had never seen). We congregated in small groups of two or three and never drew together as a group of 12, which we knew would draw attention. None of us had ever seen the ocean, flown on a plane or a ship or traveled more than 20 miles from our own village. During this time of relaxation, before the hard work of our mission began, our quiet conversations centered on the family we had left behind and what we missed about our lives before the Madrassas. We had been gone from our villages for nearly 4 years and had experienced homesickness. However, the awareness that we had traveled to an entirely different continent, had homesickness running rampant through our emotions. Not only was I the youngest, but I was feeling this loneliness even more than the others, as the burden of responsibility for the group and success of a very critical mission was weighing heavy on my shoulders. All of these factors impacted my friendship with Raga and Johey. Now my two friends, as well as the other 9 "S" cell members, treated me with distance and respect. I understood that respect for

leaders was part of our culture, but it still grabbed at my gut as I listened to the others laugh and joke with each other.
Another new experience for our group was the proximity to women, especially those scantily clothed in only bathing suits or short dresses with their heads bared. The only women we had seen back in Pakistan were covered from head to toe with burkas after they reached the age of twelve. Here sitting around the pool, we sat in awe of the young girls parading so much of their bodies in front of us. Considering our age and inexperience with the opposite sex, we stared at the girls from behind our sunglasses and when in private that night laughed and speculated about these women and what it must be like to experience the opposite sex.

On the morning of third day, I was sitting alone, by the pool reading an American travel book. Before I even saw anyone approach, I felt his presence. True to my training, I did not look up as I heard him sit in the chair next to mine. After a few moments, the man asked softly in Spanish.

"Are you Mohamed?" Although I had not expected my contact to appear in such a public place, I quickly realized this must be the man I had been waiting for.

"Yes," I replied just as quietly.

"I am 'S 15." I assume you have enjoyed your stay to my country?"

"Very much sir," I replied. Miguel seemed pleased and continued.

"Your leisure time has come to an end." This sounded like much more like a prediction of our future than just an announcement that we were leaving Puerto Cabello. Miguel, or S 15, as he introduced himself, continued.

"Tomorrow night we will leave port. A city bus will be outside your hotel at 10pm tomorrow evening. It will take you to a dock. I will meet you there. I want to warn you now, that the boat, on which you will travel, is different than any you have ever seen. You should be prepared for many different experiences.

I asked, "Can you give me more detail, so I am prepared to handle my men's reactions?"

"Oh yes, I was just getting to that," Miguel chuckled. "You are aware, Mohamed, that you and your group must arrive in America under cover of darkness. You have no passport documents to get you through customs legally, as those documents can trace your origins and at a later date, could create great harm to our cause if your group is discovered. Since 2001, Americans are on high alert watching for people that look like you."

Now, I took a close look at Miguel who appeared to be around thirty-five. He was tall and slender with jet-black hair and very tan beyond his natural olive skin. He wore a white long-sleeved shirt and long white pants, heavily starched. When he smiled, his sparkling white teeth gleamed in contrast against his dark skin, making them look brilliant.

"Mohamed, as the leader of this operation you know far more than I. My part is small but important to you. It will end when I deposit you on the American shore. I am of course a member of our al-Qaeda brotherhood. I know that you have been hand chosen by the Commander. For the safety of your mission, the details I am about to share, should remain with you alone. The other eleven members of your team will discover the method of your travels just as they are stepping off the dock into the boat."

Now I am very anxious for Miguel to reveal our plans. He continues,

Soft Target
by Larry Greer

"Tomorrow night you and your group will become a part of history. You will be boarding a boat that travels under water…a submarine. This boat is top secret and its existence is known by only a few people in the world. The majority of those involved in building this submarine were aware only of the part they played in its development. Very similar to my part in your mission, only the master planners were knowledgeable about all the unique features of this boat. I have been the test pilot from day one, and have put together a crew of myself and three others. The sub is small for any boat traveling such a distance, but it is perfectly designed for our journey. I will explain more about how it works after we get underway. We will travel, undetected, directly below a very large Brazilian freighter, The 'Zoe2. This freighter is scheduled to leave port at midnight tomorrow. We must be on board our sub and prepared to depart at exactly the same time. The "Zoe2" is 982 feet long and will be loaded with cargo containers. Her maximum speed is 21 knots, and our submarine is designed to go 21 knots, so we will have no problem keeping up with her. The trip should take about five days. Once your men become accustomed to small quarters under water, they should find these five days restful, as there will be nothing for them to do."

I pondered Miguel's revelations about the very strange boat, and thought that my parents would not recognize me now. It occurred to me that I had matured far beyond my fast approaching twenty-first birthday. These past few years had changed me from a gregarious young man to a quiet, cautious loner. I now knew that my mission involved taking the blood of the infidels and that had become a constant and sobering thought. The singularly-focused theme of my training at the camp had resulted in a fervent hate for everything western and especially for all Americans. For one brief moment, the thought occurred to me, I hated a group of people I have never seen or whose culture I only knew from my indoctrination at camp. I knew I had to let that concern go and be resolved to the truth of my mission. I had seen many classroom films developed by the AL Jazeera TV network, broadcasting Jihad speeches made by both al-Qaeda and Taliban leaders. They all professed strong and hateful words about Americans. They showed violent beheadings, stoning and mutilation of women. They said this jihad was Allah's will. As a result of all this hatred, I lived for the day when I could cast my first death blow against the infidels. Suddenly, something Miguel said came back to me as incorrect.

"Miguel, you just indicated that we will depart tomorrow night for America. My information was that we would be traveling first to Mexico and then cross the border into to America."

"Mohamed, I just received this information a few days ago. It seems that you were never intended to go to Mexico. Your superiors were protecting your team and your mission against the chance of a mole embedded in the camp. It was their intent to give your team time to get out of the country and away from the camp, before communicating the actual travel plans to you."

CHAPTER 18

Dulles Airport

The Pope's 'Shepherd One' landed at an executive hanger within Dulles Airport in Washington, D.C. on April 15th 2008. Carlos Mendias had done his job well in Vatican City. He had successfully hidden the twelve disassembled machine pistols within the body of the Pope's primary vehicle without arousing suspicion. The spare tire was always covered in a canvas bag. Carlos had taken the canvas cover home with him, inserted the outer layer of a tire inside the cover, creating a thin circle of rubber. This allowed space to conceal the pistols within the bag. It looked like a spare tire and it felt like a spare tire. Due to the lack of security and a light work force in and around the garage at the Vatican, the job had been easier than Mendias had originally thought. He finished on time and as agreed, he left a note that morning in an envelope on the seat of his truck. When he returned to his truck that evening, the envelope was gone. He never knew who picked up and delivered the envelopes and knew he was better off ignorant of this information. Two days later his phone rang. A voice he did not recognize spoke quickly in Italian,

"The Commander is pleased with your work and sends you his thanks."
The phone went dead and Mendias stared at it for a minute in surprise. This was enough for Mendias. He had been useful to the brotherhood. He smiled to himself and headed home to his wife and children.

Soft Target
by Larry Greer

On April 15th, as planned, the Pope's plane landed at a private terminal near Dulles Airport. This private arrival avoided the large crowds the Pope always attracted and saved significant security dollars. He was met by a few dozen dignitaries, and quickly swept away to his hotel suite for a good night's sleep before beginning his short American visit. The Pope traveled with extensive wardrobe and equipment. For security and convenience, all items except of course, the Pope Mobile, had been packed in containers. After releasing the straps that held the vehicle secure in the plane, it was rolled down a ramp at the rear of the plane. The gas tank had been emptied for the journey, so its first stop was the pump next to the hanger. A local mechanic with above average security clearance was assigned to check the vehicle for any issues that might have occurred in transit. This job fell to Abraham Raice. He had been shop foreman at this executive hanger for over 10 years. He got a lot of kidding about his name from those who said it must be his stage name. In a way, these taunting's were right on target. Abraham Raice was not this man's real name. It was one he had assumed when he became a member of an al Qaeda sleeper cell in Washington D.C. This was Abraham's first assignment with the brotherhood. The Pope Mobile would not be used until the next day so this gave him time to drop the spare tire lid down, remove the pistols and replace them with an actual spare tire. It was easy for him to load the pistols into his truck bed hide them under some metal and lumber scraps he had been carrying around for several weeks, in preparation for this mission.

    The next day Raice delivered the guns to another cell member. He did not know this man, but very detailed plans had been devised so that the delivery would be secure.

    Ben Wilson received the pistols without a hitch. This type of undercover job was right up his alley. He had profitably smuggled drugs from Miami for several years and had only been arrested once. Although sentenced to two years in prison, he

Soft Target
by Larry Greer

quickly discovered that good behavior would result in early release, due to crowded cells and inadequate conditions. During his time in prison, Ben had been introduced to Islam. Upon his early release, Ben converted and dropped his birth name, becoming Alee Rashid. This new name was useful in a number of ways. Rashid was an expert at smuggling. He knew which routes were the ones watched closely by the Feds. He avoided Interstate 95 which ran from Miami to Washington and was a primary route for illegal drugs, guns and human trafficking. Rashid knew all the back roads. He had devised a plan that he felt would be fool-proof.

For the purpose of this run, he found an old concrete truck at the junk yard. It was beat up but still ran. He had most of it repainted but left some of the old paint showing. The next stop was a tow truck operator, two towns away. They specialized in towing large vehicles cross country. He was certain that a concrete truck, being towed by a reputable tow truck company could head southward without arousing suspicion. Once all was in place, he called the tow truck operator and had the old concrete truck picked up. Alee had placed the pistols in a box and secured them inside the truck's large concrete holding barrel. He gave the owner of the tow trucking company three thousand dollars and the address of the junk yard where he wanted it delivered. Alee instructed, "When your driver drops the truck, have him call this number and leave a message that he has completed his delivery. The junk yard owner did not know Alee's real name or what he was actually transporting. The guns could not be traced back to anyone in America or back to Rome. All communication about this mission had been either verbal or written communication that was immediately destroyed. All phone calls had been untraceable burn phones. Every brotherhood member involved only knew his contact by an "S" number. Every detail had been covered.

CHAPTER 19

The Zoe2

Our group of twelve departed the hotel individually at various times throughout the day to avoid any suspicion. Our senses were still on overload after five days leisure and titillating new sights. We were oblivious to the tropical storm that was predicted to hit Puerto Cabello. At 9:00pm as we gathered in front of the bus stop, approaching from various directions to catch the city bus, high winds were driving the rain horizontally into our faces. Although we were the only ones on the bus, I did not speak to any of my team during the ride to the dock. As directed, I had not revealed the fact that our boat was a submarine. I knew this would make the men nervous. I was quite certain that most of the men would be both amazed and shocked by this vehicle. Heavy rain flooded the streets and several small cars were submerged halfway up their doors in floodwater. Stranded drivers had climbed on top of the vehicles in hopes of being rescued. Our driver, however, did not veer from his mission of getting us to the dock at the appointed hour. There were several big freighters in port. Not one of us had ever seen such large ships. Again we were in awe of these new experiences. Even with the storm bearing down, flood lights on the freighters illuminated huge containers being lifted with giant magnates and stacked on top of each other on the freighter. Street lights were obliterated by the driving rain, and increasingly heavy wind bowed palm trees toward the ground. Windshield wipers on the bus, struggled to clear rain from the front window, causing the driver to lose sight of the road several times, tossing us around in a manner that predicted our approaching voyage. After what seemed like eons, we approached a fenced area with imposing signs warning: 'Restricted Area'. The driver inched-open the bus door to get out and release the gate. Gale-force winds drove rain inside the bus, drenching most of us. The

Soft Target
by Larry Greer

driver could barely make it 50 feet to the gate without being blown away. I attempted to step out to help him, but he motioned me back inside. After several tries, he managed to unlock the heavy gate and force it open. Bent over to keep the rain out of his face, he lost his footing and fell several times into deep water. I held the bus door open for him to enter and it took us both to pull the door closed against the rising winds. Our bus entered the restricted area and crept slowly through the ink-like darkness of the parking lot. The bus slowed and came to a stop. All we could see were horizontal sheets of rain in the bus's headlights. The driver, still soaked from his venture to open the door, turned and silently directed us to grab our packs and follow him. Had he voiced his instructions, we could not have heard him over the impending storm.

Finally, Johey could not contain his fear any longer,
"I do not see a ship. Where have you taken us?" The driver just smiled and shouted over the rain and wind.

"Watch your step. Follow me. There are fourteen steps down to your boat. Hold very tightly onto the hand rail or you will find yourself in the ocean below."
It was a treacherous 14 steps filled with fear and uncertainty. Once all the men had safely reach the narrow dock a new voice called out in Spanish from the darkness,
"Follow me." A dim light appeared from the direction of the new voice. He held the flashlight to show the way for us to again descend a ladder that led down into the boat. Raga's jaw dropped. He could now see the outline of a strange water craft barely protruding above the two foot waves created by the storm. The voice shouted over the storm.

"Welcome aboard the 'Hugo Chavez', I am your Captain. Watch your step. Cross on the ramp one by one. Hold tightly to the rail and when you reach the hatch, you will be helped down the ladder by the first mate."

As we stood soaked to the bone by the driving rain, waiting our turn to cross the plank and descend into the boat, it felt like we would never be dry again. I boarded the 'Hugo Chavez' last. Once we were all safely in the sub, the twelve of us took in our surroundings and realized that traveling in this narrow submarine would be yet another new experience. Everything on this boat was different. It smelled metallic. It was dimly lit, to preserve power and every inch of the boat had a specific purpose. Captain Miguel interrupted our thoughts. In the enclosure of the sub, he could now talk without shouting.

"This is a tight ship. Our journey will take five days. All orders must be adhered to without question. Right now, I want each of you to find a bunk, get out of your wet clothes and climb onto it. As you can see, there is no way to navigate the boat with people standing in the walkway. The first mate, Kaleed, will show you the head and the galley. Six men can eat at a time, so we will take meals in three shifts." Your food for the journey has been prepared, and will only need to be re-heated in the microwave."

The Captain continued, "Relax for the next two hours and sleep if you can. At midnight we will pull out of port and begin our trip."

Raga whispered to me that space was really tight. He feared that some might get sick from the close quarters and the motion of the boat. He could feel the sub slapping against the dock and his stomach began to churn. He nervously wondered how much worse it could be in the open ocean.

"Just be patient Raga. All will be well," I assured him. "Remain focused on our mission."

Soft Target
by Larry Greer

Raga let his fear overtake him and shot back, "We do not even know what our mission is or where we are going. We have been trained to do many things, yet you keep us in the dark about the future."

The storm and uncertainty of our journey had me on edge as well and I responded a little too harshly, "Did you not learn that patience is a virtue? We will know more about our mission in a matter of days. I have been instructed by our leaders what I can impart to you and what I must keep to myself. It is for your security, Raja. Have some faith in your old friend."

Raja quieted after my tongue lashing. "Yes Mohamad, I understand." Although his voice was compliant, his eyes were still brooding.

In an effort to allay fears, Captain Miguel took us into the Hugo Chavez control room before leaving port. We went in groups of two or three and by the time two groups had experienced the technology capabilities of this boat, word of mouth had the entire team excited about the journey. His tactic worked. Captain Miguel then imparted his next instructions. Each team member received pencil and paper. We were told the five days would require total silence. All communication would be made through notes to each other. The Captain explained that American Subs in the area could hear the tiniest sounds through sonar technology. Again we were amazed and dumbfounded. So many new experiences! It began to dawn on me for the second time that day. We would never be going back to our homes and families. Our lives had changed forever.

At five minutes before midnight, Miguel told me that the 'Zoe2" was beginning to move out of port in spite of the storm. Our rule of absolute silence began at that moment. The sub began maneuvering out into the dark swirling waters. Soon we felt the sub descend and the impact of the storm abated. We slowly dropped to a depth of 20-meters . After about an hour, Kaleed produced a document which detailed how the sub functioned. He indicated on a note, that he could answer any questions we wanted to write down and give him. Each man read the document and passed it on to the next man. After several hours, the fear and excitement of the journey was overcome by fatigue. Men took to their bunks and quickly dozed off to the droning sound of the powerful 'Zoe2' engines that were only about fifty feet above. Captain Miguel could see the outline of the big freighter on his monitor. Instruments recorded their depth below the freighter as well as their relative speeds. Even Miguel was amazed by how quiet the small 'Hugo Chavez' ran.

The next day we began falling into a routine. I told the men in a note that they must take turns laying in the aisle and doing exercises. This was critical in order to maintain our strength. The four crew members took 6-hour shifts. Their job was demanding, as we had to maintain speed that kept us directly under the 'Zoe2' without being detected. The crew could not allow any mistakes.

On day three the 'Zoe2' began to drop speed and our crew could detect that the freighter had cut off its engines. Miguel did the same and cut all lights in the sub to maintain battery power. All was darkness and silence for the men. Time also seemed to stop. Miguel donned his ear phones. Now he could hear voices on the 'Zoe2' above him. The voices were not totally clear, but from the conversation, he calculated it must be the captain speaking. What he realized was that the 'Zoe2' captain was talking to the captain of an American sub nearby. The 'Zoe2' Captain was being informed that there was an anomaly near his ship. The Captain of the American sub surmised it could be a whale following the freighter, but that was not normal activity for whales. The

Soft Target
by Larry Greer

American sub Captain went on to say that whatever it was, it was completely silent. The 'Zoe2' Captain questioned if it could be another sub. He was told, this was doubtful because of the small size of the image on sonar. Besides, the American sub could detect the engine noise of another sub propelling through the water. With this information, the 'Zoe2' captain concurred, that whatever it was, it was not a threat to him. He thanked the American sub captain and indicated he would restart his engines and continue toward New Orleans, since the storm's wind had put him behind schedule.

    Captain Miguel decided if he moved the Hugo Chaves closer to the hull of the 'Zoe2', any small degree of interference from his sub would be picked up as part of the freighter's mass. In Miguel's mind, this would create an integrated blur on the big US subs radar and throw them off. The 'Zoe2' was again on its way and Miguel detected no more conversations with the American sub. Miguel then passed a note to Mohamed, explaining what had happened. Each of the men, upon reading the note, felt the danger they could be entering.

    Was it really possible that the Americans had such advanced technology? This was even going through my mind as I thought about what was ahead for our team. I pondered the possibilities while I lay in my bunk. I attempted sleep, but it would not come. My mind began to wander back to childhood and my village of Jiba. My childhood had not been like most boys in my village. The friends I had made as a young boy grew up with normal experiences in Jiba. But since the age of 15, I had been in intense training for a mission that had not yet been revealed. I thought about my mother and father. I thought fondly of my brother. What was their life like? There had been no communication between us in over a year. I hoped they were benefitting from the pension that had been promised as a result of my service. Finally these musings about home and family brought sleep to my tired body.

CHAPTER 20

Langley, Virginia

April 2008 had rolled around, and it had been almost three months since the Foreign Intelligence Surveillance Act known as the FISA law, had been reenacted. As suspected, it had handcuffed John Massey's Call Center. They had been very limited in their ability to identify suspected terrorist calls. By the time they could contact a FISA judge for approval to implement eavesdropping, the caller had long since ended the call. The opposition party in Congress felt they had won a skirmish with the Republican president. The country's inability to effectively manage homeland security made the President look ineffective. The second group delighted with this FISA law was the al Qaeda jihad group. It was as if they had a secret cell operating within the American Congress.

John Massey was entering his office building on Monday morning when his cell phone rang.

"John Massey," he answered.

"John, this Shelly, thought you'd want a heads up that the 'big potato' is in your office waiting for you to arrive. Impatiently, I might add."

"Thanks Shelly, I will be there in five minutes."

Soft Target
by Larry Greer

John was thinking, what could be so important that Milton would fight morning DC traffic to see me in person when a secure video conference was so much easier? John had been available all weekend, but nothing out of the ordinary had been reported. He respected Milton, who had earned his stripes the hard way. To John's knowledge, Milton had not allowed himself to be the pundit for any political cause or party. He was nearing fifty-five and John assumed that Milton must be thinking about retirement. Not that he wanted Milton gone, but John hoped he might have a chance at the Director's job when Milton did retire.

As John approached his office, he could see the door was open. Milton was sitting in the visitor's chair reading the Washington Post. John could detect his impatience, because Milton kept crossing and re-crossing his legs.
"Good morning Milton, what a nice surprise!"

Milton put down the newspaper. "And a good morning to you, John. Guess I should have called before dropping in on you, but just needed a little detour. It's been awhile since I have visited your Call Center. So how are things going?"

John knew this was a loaded question and was trying to read Milton's face. He knew Milton would not just drop by for an idle chat. John closed the door and slowly hung his coat on the back as he was figuring out how candid and how political to be with Milton.

"Well to be very candid Milt, it's been strangely quiet for the past two months. Other than the Pope's visit to Washington, there has been nothing. We are not even seeing demonstrations in front of the White House. I'm not sure if there is really nothing going on or we are just not hearing it. You know since that surveillance act passed several months ago, our hands have been tied. It is damn frustrating. I just hope that other agencies are not as constrained." Milton cleared his throat.

"John, that's what I wanted to talk with you about. According to the Pentagon, our Eastern intel feels that something is brewing. It isn't anything they can put their fingers on, but it is just too damn quiet. Unofficially, they are hoping that if you do hear anything over the lines that you might 'accidently' overlook the FISA. What I am sharing is of course, off the record. I will deny it if it ever comes up, but this is why I paid you a personal visit. This suggestion can't be recorded in any way."

Now John understood the purpose and urgency of Milton's visit. He also knew that Milton was placing him in a very awkward position. He felt strongly that although illegal, given the new law, it was however, a patriotic decision. He was glad that he and Milton shared that viewpoint. Most intel workers were former military and shared the same political views. However, there was a large component of folks in Washington that did not.

"Understood." was all John needed to say.

"Can you share more about what the Pentagon is watching?"

"From what I have been told, one of our satellites picked up a group of men who it appears have been moving out of Pakistan and into South America. They were seen boarding a cruise ship in Islamabad for Ad Dawhah in Qatar. According to a mole, they then boarded a plane for Caracas, Venezuela. We have not had word of them after that.
I'm not sure this means anything, but the CIA is watching Mexico closely. They are convinced that al-Qaeda is making plans to get across the border hidden among the many illegal Mexican crossings."

Soft Target
by Larry Greer

The mention of Islamabad caused John to remember a quick call they had picked up only yesterday.

"Not sure if this is connected, but we did pick up on a call yesterday between Washington and Islamabad. The only comment we could decipher was something about the Pope had landed and everything was fine. After that comment, they hung up, and of course, it was too short for us to put a tracer on it."

Milton looked puzzled for a moment. "Wonder what they could mean by,
'And everything is fine'?
"I don't know Milt, but I am convinced that there are far more of these people in our country than we realize and especially more in Washington."

Milton agreed. "I think you are absolutely right John, but out hands are tied on profiling. It is just not smart. This politically-correct shit is going to get us all killed." Milton stood and headed for the door. He stops suddenly, turned and directed.

"You send me anything you pick up on, no matter how short the conversation. Don't e-mail it to me. Do it the old fashioned way. Put it on paper and have a courier deliver it. Understand?" I nodded. "We don't want to get blind sided *again*." With that he turned and left, shutting the door behind him. John just sat and contemplated this conversation. A lot to digest, John thought.

A week later, Milton called John to arrange a lunch meeting.

Soft Target
by Larry Greer

"John, meet me at the Red Onion." John agreed to meet him there about 12:15pm. "I wonder what Milton wants to talk about now?" John thought.

The Red Onion was a small neighborhood sandwich shop. There were only a few tables and it wasn't a place that Washington bureaucrats hung out so John figured Milton felt comfortable talking freely in this environment. Milton asked for the back corner table.

"I have a hunch that something is going down John, but it's just a hunch. There's no solid intel to back it up."
"Tell me what have you heard?" John asks. He had known Milton for a long time and trusted his hunches.

"A highly confidential Pentagon report indicated that a U.S. nuke-sub is reporting unusual phenomena in the Gulf of Mexico. They say they cannot determine what it is because of the small size displayed on the sonar. No sound can be detected, so it doesn't appear to be another sub. The most unusual and disturbing piece of the intel is that whatever it is, it's running very close to the bottom of a big tanker named the 'Zoe2'. At the point of first detection, the U.S. sub asked the tanker captain to shut down his engines and halt progress. Now here is what is weird. Whatever it is, stopped as well."

"Do you have any thoughts what this might be, Milt?" John's curiosity is piqued. He knew Milton's hunch might provide some insight.

Milton continued, "The captain of the sub says that it is about the size of a Gray Whale on the radar, but it is not normal behavior for a whale to follow a ship for the length of time they have tracked this, 'whatever it is'. Besides, whales emit communication sounds that can be picked up. I guess it is mute now, though."

"How so?" John asks.
"Well, last night, we received an update that the tanker had entered the Port of New Orleans. If this was indeed a sub, it could not continue to follow underneath the tanker because the water would be too shallow. Once in the harbor, they lost track of it on radar. There was some speculation around the table that it could be a small sub. There are reports of drawings of small submarines that would fit this description, but to our knowledge, none have been built or tested. The other fact that makes us believe that it was not a sub is that there was no engine noise, whatsoever."

John pondered, as he took a bite of his burger.

"Milt, do you see some kind of pattern here? Last week you told me about detection of a group of men moving from Islamabad to Venezuela. Then we lost track of them."

"What's your point?"
"Well, this is highly speculative, but what if it was a sub bringing in these men from Pakistan by way of Venezuela?" At this, Milton let out a chuckle,
"Now that really would be speculative wouldn't it?" John looked back at Milton with a grin,
"You are right, that really would be beyond belief." John was reading Milton's thoughts,

"OK starting now I am going to focus a few of my team on New Orleans communication area and see if we pick up anything unusual. You know, we hadn't better take these al Qaeda guys for granted. They are real cagy about the way they communicate, making it difficult for us to get and decipher their messages. Sure wish we could get the wireless phone companies to make it difficult to use these untraceable cell phones. Problem for us is that there is no law against their use, and the companies are profit driven."

CHAPTER 21

New Orleans, Louisiana

At 2:36 am, the 'Hugo Chavez' slowly moved out from under the 'Zoe2' and crept close to the bottom of the harbor, edging towards some private docks to the east. Miguel's sophisticated navigational instruments were still able to pick up the Zoe2's satellite map, and he could tell where he was in relation to the big tanker. Miguel moved the mini sub ever so cautiously through the dark murky waters. His gyrocompass read seventy-one meters deep. He now felt safe to activate the sonar to avoid any collisions that might alert other ships or subs in the area. When he had maneuvered the sub to within 120 feet of the pier, he stopped dead in the water. He let the boat rise slowly to the surface. The sub had been built without a conning tower to accommodate the low profile design. This is what had allowed it to evade detection as a submarine. The craft would have to emerge about two feet out of the water before the main hatch could open. Miguel sent a message back to the men to ready themselves for departure. It took only four minutes for the sub to rise high enough in the water to open the hatch. It was now 3:25a.m., and the satellite showed there were no boats moving about. Kaleed went up the ladder first and turned the hatch wheel above his head. This was his responsibility as first mate. The hatch was heavy. It was extremely difficult to turn this circular wheel. With great effort, the hatch slowly began to open. Water began pouring into the boat. Slowly, it dissipated and the waterfall was replaced with the odor of dank sea air. Adrenalin began to begin to flow among the men. They knew they were about to set foot on American soil. This was a continuation of so many unknowns for these rural Pakistanis . Fear, anticipation and determination filled their thoughts. Kaleed whispered down to the crewman below him to tell the Captain to move the vessel forward about seventy meters and stop. The sub slid into an empty slip and Kaleed could actually reach out and touch dock. Using a hand winch designed to attach a boat to the dock; he could then slowly and silently pull the craft next to the dock. He had practiced this procedure many times in his training.

The lights on the dock were dimmed by the fog. Kaleed kept his eyes peeled, but did not see any movement. He did notice lights on a yacht three slips down from where they were moored, he could not detect movement. He surmised that the occupants were out late and had not returned. After several tries, Kaleed was able to latch his ropes to the dock. Slowly the sub came along side the pier. Upon securing the sub as close to the dock as possible, he attached a rope ladder for the men to climb onto the pier, one man at a time.

Johey was the first up the ladder. He quickly looked in all directions, but there was no one in sight. He motioned for the others to follow. They had been instructed to make the ascent out of the boat as quickly and silently. As each one took his place at the bottom of the sub's ladder, Miguel shook their hand. He would not be leaving the sub. His mission was to prepare his sub to follow another freighter back to Caracas, early the next day. He was thinking how good it felt to have completed his mission. However, he had a gut feeling that this was perhaps just the first of many crossings from Caracas to America.

Mohamad directed his team to disperse into the shadows. They knew to remain close until their contact showed up. Mohamad would move slowly to the end of the pier, always staying in the shadows. It was here he would wait. To thwart any moles in their cell, the plan had been changed just before leaving Caracas. Originally he was to head into town, and call his contact from the closest phone booth. That was determined to be too risky. Now, the signal would be a man lighting a cigarette…easy to spot in the darkness. The sound of music, coming from one of the nearby yachts faded in and out. In the distance a man and woman could be heard arguing with each other. Mohamed reached his destination. He sat down on a cargo box in the shadows and waited. His watch read 4:03am. The sun would begin to peek over the horizon at exactly 6:35 this morning. The pungent smell of rotting fish and trash mingled with the humid air on the harbor. Although Mohamed was used to sewage smells in Jiba, this was a new foul odor. New Orleans was still a pile of garbage, even two years after Hurricane Katrina. Sharp claws of the rats could be heard scurrying along the dock as they rummaged through trash. Mohamed's eyes had finally adjusted, and he could watch these huge rodents running in and out of small openings in the walls of the pier. Suddenly the sound of footsteps nearby stirred him from his focus on the rats. The sound would stop for a few moments and then resume. Each time this happened, the sound was closer. Mohamed remained rigid not wanting to be discovered if the person approaching was not his contact. He feared being detected by police. He automatically placed his hand over the handle of the knife that rested inside his right boot. He tested the ease of its release from the sheaf to ensure he could react quickly if necessary. He had received the most thorough self-defense training possible and had no doubt about his ability to swiftly take another man out in complete silence. Mohamed's chest tightened. He was sure that the deafening beat of his heart would give him away. Still, he remained motionless. Now, the steps had come to a stop. They sounded very close. Total silence! Then from the corner of his eye he heard the faintest click of a lighter and he saw the faint glow of a tiny flame on the other side of the crates that separated him from the cigarette-smoking stranger. He hoped with all his heart that this person was his contact. He remained completely

Soft Target
by Larry Greer

silent, except for his deafening heartbeat. Quietly, a very deep voice emanated from across the crates.

"S One, are you near?"

Mohamed silently stood. He recognized the question as his code signal and felt confident that this man was his contact. He slowly peered around the crates. The profile of a man stood about twelve feet from him. The man was staring in the opposite direction. It was too dark to see a glimpse of his face but his slightly stooped stance made him seem older. Mohamed's training kicked in. Suspicion and caution guided his every move these days, so it was with reluctance that he finally responded with a quite acknowledgement, "Yes."

At this acknowledgment, the man turned toward Mohamed. Neither could see the other's face in the foggy darkness. The man began speaking in English,

"I am called Hernando. I am here to lead you and your men to a safe house and direct you on your journey north. Do you prefer English or Spanish?"

"English" responded Mohamed, and so the man continued.
"Are the rest of your men nearby?"
"Yes."

"Then I want you to instruct them to make their way in pairs of two, in the shadows to the pier gate. There is no security at this gate for the next hour. I will be waiting for you there."

Mohamed nodded and made his way back down the pier to where his crew was waiting. When he figured they were all in earshot, he gave a short bird call. They began to appear out of the darkness. In a whisper, instructed them to follow each other one by one. He would lead and he directed Johey to be the sweep,

Soft Target
by Larry Greer

ensuring no member of the team wandered in the wrong direction. He warned that if they encountered anyone else on the pier, they were to look away, laugh and speak in their best Spanish. That way they would be taken for Mexicans. With that, Mohamed stepped out with Raga at his side. As they passed the lighted yacht they met two women and two young men obviously drunk, coming their way swinging beer bottles. These two couples did not seem to even notice them as they passed each other. It was to be the first Americans the highly trained terrorist had seen. Once at the gate, Mohamed could see Hernando across the street standing next to a dingy yellow school bus with the school's name crudely over painted by lettering that read 'Local Produce' After Hurricane Katrina, hundreds of aging busses had been donated to the flood-ravaged New Orleans area. Since that time many had languished in this water-front parking lot. A number of the buses had been purchased by small businesses. Traveling through the French Quarter of New Orleans now, you would see dozens of these decrepit vehicles. Hernando motioned for them to cross the street and board the bus. Mohamed stopped each pair of men as they approached to make sure all was o.k. and then directed them toward the bus, each time checking to making sure there were no cars approaching. Once all were aboard, Hernando turned the key and the rough engine noise was the first thing in America that reminded them of their home far-away in Pakistan. Mohamed placed himself directly behind the driver. Keeping his head facing the road, Hernando told Mohamed that his first stop would be the early morning farmers market. He said that should they be stopped, he would look legitimate carrying fresh produce and "local farm workers". Both men knew that the dark coloring of the Afghan men would serve them well in New Orleans.

At the market Hernando stopped the bus near other similar vehicles and ordered Mohamed to have the men stay in the bus, remain quiet and keep their heads down. When he returned, he was accompanied by two more men, carrying crates of produce. They

Soft Target
by Larry Greer

were placed at the front of the bus, where the first several rows of seats had been removed for that purpose. He left again and after about 15 minutes reappeared with the same two men carrying more produce. Before they could finish loading crates from the second trip, Mohamed noticed a policeman heading their direction. His heartbeat quickened and softly hushed his men. The policeman peered through the dirty windows noticing the men. He turned to Hernando and asked,

"Why you have so many 'beaners' on your bus?" Hernando quickly responded,
"They are paying me to take them to the sugar fields."
"Are they 'border bunnies' or do they have green cards?", the policeman inquired.

"I guess they do. Why don't you ask them yourself," Hernando bravely suggested. Mohamed held his breath. The policeman stepped up into the bus and took a long look at the twelve men and asked,

"Do you 'beaners' have green cards?" Mohamed jumped to answer in his best Spanglish.

"Si, senior. Would you like to see them?" The officer appeared to not want to go to the trouble of checking green cards. He shook his head and backed off the bus. New Orleans, decades ago had become a sanctuary city. This meant that unless there appeared to be an obvious problem, the police did not hassle the "brown people".

Hernando boarded the bus and expertly wove it thought the narrow streets leaving the historic Crescent City Farmers Market. The men caught their first glimpse of the city as the soft light of early morning began to dust the New Orleans skyline. Still nervous, Mohamed leaned forward and whispered to Hernando,

Soft Target
by Larry Greer

"That was close." Hernando chortled and replied,
"Not <u>even</u> close. That policeman is a friend of mine. He was just making it appear that he was doing his job."

It was only then that my breathing slowed to normal. I sat back in my seat and relaxed a little. I felt a new sense of confidence in Hernando. My body was exhausted and my emotions were spent …our first few hours in America! However, my curiosity won out. I wanted to see the city. It felt gigantic, with ornate tall buildings and more trees than any of us had ever seen. Trees in my part of the world were scrubby and brown. Green was not a color we were familiar with. We watched trolleys slowing at intersections and people gracefully jumped on board and hung out at an angle as the trolley resumed its slow journey along the wire path overhead. Everything we saw was new and stimulating. Soon we turned onto a very wide smooth road, where cars and trucks were flying by at a speed that seemed extremely dangerous. Hernando told us this was called an Interstate Highway. It connected the vast regions of America so that people could travel anywhere in the United States. The team was in awe of this amazing road and their mouths were agape as they read the big green road signs in English. At last the weariness of my body overtook the excitement of our new environment and I fell into a shallow, fitful sleep.

Soft Target
by Larry Greer

CHAPTER 22

Langley, Virginia

The secure phone on John Massey's desk rang. John knew this meant trouble. He picked it up and Milton's voice on the other end of the line emanated a sense of urgency.
"John, I need you at the Pentagon immediately." All John could think, was 'oh, shit'.

"What is it Milt?"
"We have an important G1 teleconference with the Navy at exactly zero nine-hundred. I want you to hear this first hand."
"Yes Sir," John automatically responded.

It would have been helpful, John thought, if Milton would have been a little more forthcoming, but that was the way Milton operated. He knew this would be a tough drive in the mid-morning traffic. Luck would have to be on his side. When he crossed over the Arlington Bridge into Washington, John could see he would never make it on his own. A Capital City Police car was parked at the side of the road, having just finished administering a ticket. John pulled in behind him. He walked over to the cop, showed his credentials and gave him enough information about the situation that the cop agreed to clear traffic with his blue light. As he pulled into the Pentagon lot, he waved a thank you to the officer and again showed his creds to the guard. He now only had five minutes. He took the steps two at a time, with his creds still in his hand. John knew the drill: the creds; the visual confirmation by the guard; and finally the thumb print. The door clicked and John walked into building. He sprinted the distance toward the media room. Only one more check point and he'd be there. John entered the room and noticed Milton's expression changed to one of relief.

"I didn't think you'd make it. We heard there is a huge jam on the Arlington Bridge." John let a small grin slip from his lips and told Milton,
"Got a little resourceful." At that minute a Navy Admiral stood up in front of the group and cleared his voice.
"Ladies and Gentlemen, in a few moments we will be getting a report from one of our nuclear submarines. This report will be top secret, so disclosure of the sub or its whereabouts will not be part of this report.

John quickly checked out the room. Wow, a lot of brass. Milton had obviously created a temporary top security clearance for him or he would not be in this room. When the Admiral stopped speaking, the men went silent in anticipation. The room was dimly lit with significant electronics and telecommunication equipment. It was known in the Pentagon as the Bridge Room and was usually reserved for top brass only. Static, then colored bars lit up the oversized screen at the front of the room. Admiral Sally Robb, spoke up. This is G1. Are we clear? Sally was the first woman to become a Navy Admiral and most recently had been appointed by the President to Secretary of Defense
Although a voice could be heard on the screen, video portion of the equipment remained off. "I can hear you fine." Secretary of Defense, Robb continued,

"I understand that you have information about unusual activity around your sub. Proceed."

John had a pen and pad in his hand, prepared to take notes. Milton put his hand on the pad, shaking his head. John immediately understood that nothing was to be recorded. The sub's Captain began,

"Gentlemen...ladies...some of you may be aware of an unusual sighting in the Gulf of Mexico about five days ago. At that time, we could not identify the anomaly on the radar screen. What we do know is that, whatever it was plotted exactly the same route from Caracas as a tanker that recently landed in the New Orleans Port. We lost it at that point and assumed it changed course due to the shallow water in the harbor. However, we now suspect that it proceeded into port either beneath or near to the tanker, as impossible as that seems. We have most recently detected a similar object located near the vicinity of another large tanker with Caracas as its destination. Today, our sub moved to within one hundred yards of the blip on our radar screen. Not wanting to break silence we did not turn on our sonar. We did however pick up a strange magnetic field unrelated to the tanker that was navigating the same route as the tanker and moving at the same exact speed. This time, we picked up a very faint hum. We are confident that this the sound of a large number of high-powered batteries. We have very carefully taken measurements from three sides and estimate the object is approximately 110 feet in length with a 14 foot beam and 9 feet in height. We believe this is a highly experimental small submarine. Our plan is to continue following the tanker and the other craft at a safe distance to avoid detection. We will report any new developments and await your direction."

Secretary Robb responded,
"Captain, do you have an opinion about either the origin or the mission of this submarine?"

"Madam Secretary, We assume it originated in Caracas, but have no proof. We surmise that it might have attached its route to the tanker to remain undetected and perhaps made a delivery into the United States…possibly delivering subversives into the country." The Secretary interrupted,

"Captain, are you familiar with any submarines of this size? Could it be a private vessel? Have you been able to detect any voices or other decipherable sounds?"
"I am not aware of any private subs of this size. I am aware of some experimental battery operated boats, but nothing has been developed that could travel this distance as without recharging batteries. As far as voices go, they are moving in total silence."

The Secretary instructed the Captain to let her know immediately of any additional developments. With that, the Secretary of Defense disconnected the call and directed her comments to the room,

"The Captain's opinion is disturbing. Since we have no urgent issues with the Venezuelans I can only surmise that any terrorists deposited into New Orleans, would have been traveling through Caracas from, most likely the Middle East. As of this moment, Homeland Security is on alert. All other branches of the military will be notified. Milton, your people should be profiling Arabs in and around New Orleans. If terrorists were deposited in New Orleans from that sub, they could be heading anywhere by now. The Secretary dismissed the gathering and directed her comments to Milton.
"Milton, I need a word with you. Please remain." Milton nodded for John to leave with the others. The Secretary continued after everyone had cleared the room.

"Milton, this is off the record, but necessary. I want your department to bypass FASA. I will take the hit if it comes to that. I have a strong hunch that the sub Captain was onto something. I have a hunch that they are depositing infiltrators into this country. I also feel strongly that this vessel is connected to al Qaeda and we have to find out what they are up to, whoever "they" really are."

"Yes Madam Secretary. I'm experiencing some of the same hunches based on some communications we have seen come through recently. Of course, because of FASA, we weren't fast enough to track the communication. Now that our handcuffs are loosened, we can be more of an asset."

Soft Target
by Larry Greer

CHAPTER 23

North of New Orleans

The Produce bus with the 'S' team aboard turned off the Freeway that had taken them many miles north of New Orleans. Hernando turned left onto a sandy dirt road pitted with potholes. As the bus bounced with each rain-filled hole, muddy water sprayed over the bus and some into the open windows. I was jarred awake. Checking my watch I saw that it was almost 9:00am. I had slept fitfully for almost four hours. Out the window, the landscape was painted with a thousand different shades of green. What a difference from the city we left. There were no tall buildings or even houses among the trees that hung out over the road. And draping from the branches of these trees, were long grey strands that reminded me of the beards of our elders and the warm air felt claustrophobic. After a few minutes, when the sleep had left my head, I asked Hernando where we were headed.

"Two years ago a great storm, they named Katrina, left thousands of our people homeless. The Government brought in hundreds and hundreds of small portable homes for temporary shelter. After a few months, many people were able to rebuild their homes or left the area altogether and the trailers were left vacant. I bought ten of them and set them up as rentals for people who come to fish the river. When the brotherhood gave me this assignment, I purchased four more trailers and moved them to a location that would be private. This is a very deserted area. No people live close by. You and your team will be able to rest here until I can arrange your transportation further north. You will have everything you need in these trailers. I have supplied them with fresh food and you will take the produce I bought this morning. Although there are bathrooms in the buildings, they are not yet plumbed. You can bath in the small river that runs behind the trailers and use the outhouses at the back. When you are outside, I suggest that you stay on the back side so if anyone drives by, they will not see you. I will come and check on you every few days and give you the latest news."

Outhouses? This was a term I had not heard before.

The bus turned left onto a short road that lead up to a series of metal buildings that were spaced out about one hundred feet apart. Hernando opened the door and the heat and humidity of Southern Louisiana, accosted them on every front. The air was thick with humidity and small biting insects everywhere. In Pakistan, the air was dry, but here it was sticky. Hernando showed them around. Noticing their aversion to the "no-seeums" he made a point of showing the men how to use the cans of bug spray he had supplied. The two charcoal grills were a novelty to the men. And he took time showing two of them how to fire up the charcoal. He had also supplied Mexican tortillas, which were the closest thing to the bread they were used to in Pakistan.

Hernando told me that if anyone came poking around asking questions he gave me a business card with his number and I should call him. They had all the necessary documents indicating they were here legally, so there should not be any problems. "Just say that you are here to work in the sugar cane fields and they can contact me for details. And remember to speak only Spanish with a little broken English," Hernando instructed.

The next few days passed slowly, as the men had nothing to do. The humidity sapped their strength and they spent lazy afternoons in the shade of the large oak trees. These trees, like the ones along the road, were covered, as I had learned, with Spanish moss. The next time Hernando visited, he had newspapers and books. I had asked Hernando to bring reading material that would bring me up to date on current events in America. I was especially interested in all that was written about illegal Mexicans coming across the border. The reading material confirmed what I suspected, many were finding their way into the Southeast where jobs were plentiful and when they were caught, in most cases, they were released back into the general population within twenty-four hours. The jails were already full and the public officials did not want to fool with them. All this would work to the 'S'teams advantage. What I did not know, was that Homeland Security had put out a secret directive to start profiling the "brown people" as we were all classified.

CHAPTER 24

The Target

On the day before we left the training camp in Northern Pakistan, we were told that only bin Laden had the target of the 'S'team's mission. We were informed that each player in this jihad knew only their part of the puzzle. Because the 911 attacks had not been as successful as al Qaeda had planned, they were now being even more secretive. Eventually, someone would soon have to tell me final details of the plan so that I could carry out bin Laden's wishes. I knew that this would have to be one of bin Laden's most trusted insiders.

After one week at the little trailer park amid the swamps of Louisiana, Hernando sat one afternoon with Mohamed alone told him the preparations for the next leg of their journey. He should let his team know they would be on the road again soon. Hernando explained,

"What we will to do is to take you, one at a time, to a bus station that is located in a little town near here called Ponchatoula. This is a location where a lot of Mexicans are dropped off to work in the sugar fields. Many of the workers travel north into the Carolinas looking for later crops or better full-time jobs. Your team will follow that path. Each of your team will be given a map and they are to work their way up to a small city in South Carolina known as Clemson. There will be no markings on the map that shows a specific route to Clemson, South Carolina. Each team member will need to commit the route to memory. Their travel should be done one by one, not even in groups of two. Individually, each man can blend in with a small group of Mexicans in the fields or on a bus and not attract attention. The Mexicans will know that you are not one of them. However, it will be believable, if your men explain that they lived in Mexico many years and wanted a better life in America, just like them. If they are stopped, they will have the green card along with other documents that will show that they came from Mexico. Upon arriving in South Carolina, each man will call a phone number that I am passing around. It too should be committed to memory. This call should be made from a pay phone at the Clemson bus station. The recorded voice on the phone will give you an address close by. Take a cab from the bus station. Mohamed, you should be first to go. There is a bus that travels this route 4 times each day, so all of you should arrive in Clemson within thirty-six hours of each other. The first bus ticket you purchase will be from Ponchatoula to Atlanta, Georgia. Once in Atlanta, buy another ticket to Clemson, South Carolina. This should reduce any suspicions at the small Ponchatoula bus station. When you are buying your ticket I suggest you get in line behind one or more Mexicans. I understand you have been provided with sufficient currency to get you to this next leg of your journey. Is that correct? Hernando asked.

Mohamed nodded and pondered the many things that could go wrong with his men all split up and traveling individually.

Soft Target
by Larry Greer

CHAPTER 25

The Old Cement Mixer

Ol' Man Harper, as his friends called him, had been retired from trucking for about three years now. His wife passed away the a little more than a year ago and he mostly passed the time by hanging out with his friend Harry, at his junkyard. Jack Harper and Harry Potts had known each other since high school, so these days when the junk yard was not busy, there was a lot of fat to chew between the two of them. Jack had kept his commercial driver's license current so he could do short trips and earn a little extra money. He liked to keep these short jaunts in and around the Washington D.C. area. Jack stopped by the junk yard to have coffee and smoke a few 'cigs' with Harry, as he did most mornings. Harry was nowhere to be found so Jack just settled in an old chair outside the office and waited. Finally, Harry emerged from the back of the garage and called out to Jack.

"Ol' Man, I have a real job for you if you are interested."

"And just what would that be Harry?"

"I need someone to take my big 'Peterbuilt' wrecker to Georgetown and pick up an old cement mixer, then deliver it to South Carolina."

"Oh man, all the way down to South Carolina? You know I don't like long-haul jobs, Harry." Jack replied, in an exaggerated whine. He figured Harry must be kidding. His work was always local.

"That's about a five or six hundred mile trip. It would be 'perty' money." Harry teased.

"You're darn-tootin' it's over five hundred miles." Jack fired back. "That's at least four days, round trip." Harry taunted John.

"Think you could be up for it? That's good money!"

"Does a cat have a tail? Hell, yes, I would I'll do it if you are gonna pay me what I'm worth."

"Fine, I will pay you eight hundred dollars plus any expense and of course you can use the company credit card for fuel."

"You did not say where in South Carolina."

"It's a place called Clemson. Ever hear of it?"
"Are you kidding? That's the home of Hartwell College…my favorite college team. I just might wander over to the stadium and take a gander. What's your delivery deadline for that cement mixer?"

"If you go get the mixer in Georgetown tomorrow, you can bring it back here so we can check tires. I don't need my Peterbilt in a pile up because the mixer had a blowout. You could probably leave for South Carolina day after tomorrow and get there on time for the delivery."

"You got it, Harry." Jack was excited about having something different to fill his day. Coffee with Harry, working in

Soft Target
by Larry Greer

his garden and sitting in his tattered easy chair, and remembering the past was taking its toll on his attitude.

Soft Target
by Larry Greer

CHAPTER 26

The Journey into South Carolina

Before leaving his team, Mohamed thoroughly briefed them about how each one would make the trip north to South Carolina. They rehearsed the instructions and the Clemson phone number among themselves until Mohamed was convinced that they were ready. Hernando had chosen Sunday morning for Mohamed to begin his journey to Clemson. Sundays were the day many of the farm workers and their families traveled from one area to another. This allowed them to be in the new fields early on Monday mornings. Because he was still nervous about leaving his team, Mohamed spoke with each man individually. He again grilled them about the details they were to remember. They were to blend in with the farm workers. They were to wear their shorts below the knee as many of the young Mexicans did. They were to wear their ball caps on backwards if they saw others do it. If they had an encounter with a policeman, they were to look him in the eye, otherwise they were to avoid eye contact and remain as inconspicuous as possible. They were to remember their Mexican history, where they were supposed to have lived in Mexico and family names. He emphasized that they were to rehearse all this information in their mind repeatedly. They must be convincing and must remember their Spanish name. And finally he reminded them that it would be dangerous for them to be seen observing their daily prayers. Allah was aware of their mission and knew faithfulness was in their hearts.

CHAPTER 27

Upstate Louisiana

Early Friday morning Sheriff Joe Dillsworth sat in his modest office on Main Street in the small town of Ponchatoula, Louisiana. It was already hot, and the humidity was threatening to be unbearable yet again. He wanted another coffee, but knew it would make more sense to drink water. He hated water and decided on a coke. The sweat was beginning to bead up on his round face. A large consumption of beer last night left him looking bloated this morning. Ponchatoula was more of a crossroads than a town. The population was a little less than 600. The biggest excitement in the Sheriff's Office was usually local boys getting drunk and shooting out the road signs. These good ol' boys also liked to harass the migrant Mexican farm workers. These local boys wanted him to interrogate every one of them because they were sure they were illegals. Sherriff Joe knew it would do no good to lock them up because Immigration officers would never charge them and he just ended up having to feed these 'beaners' and their families. It was easier to just leave them be as they made their way from one field to the next. Sheriff Joe knew that the farmers needed the Mexicans because they would work for a lower wage than the Americans and they really did work hard. When the farmer was required to provide housing, the Mexicans would all pile into one hovel and that saved the farmer money too. Neither the black or white farm workers would do that. Because many of the farmers were influential in the community, Joe and his two deputies chose to look the other way.

Soft Target
by Larry Greer

It was a quiet Friday morning and Joe was bored. He was scrolling through his email, only half paying attention because he hated this machine. In an attempt to keep up with the times, the city council had demanded Joe become computer literate. He couldn't believe that these three housewives and four old retired coots knew how to work a computer themselves. Most of his email was what he considered junk; people complaining about this or that. All of a sudden something caught his eye. --- *'Urgent'* From *Homeland Security* --- He clicked on it and read:

This is a national alert--- There is reason to believe that there have been illegal aliens coming in through the Port of New Orleans as recently as the last few weeks. Although they could be posing as Hispanics, it is believed that they could be South Americans or Arabs. They may be armed and dangerous. Surveillance of all bus, train and airports must have high priority. Any detained person of interest must be held for the Immigration authorities. As a reminder, local law enforcement is subject to the federal law that requires you to release any suspect that cannot be lawfully charged within twenty four hours. Federal and regional Immigration phone numbers are listed below. Post these numbers and provide the information for all local law enforcement personnel. Attached are photos of several nationalities including Hispanics and Arabs. Make sure your staff is familiar with the demographic differences.

Sheriff Joe Dillsworth was leaning back in his rickety chair and thinking how complicated law enforcement jobs are in the big cities. He could not even envision that the type of people described in this email, would come to his little town of Ponchatoula. However, he thought, we do have a bus station and the passengers on those busses are mostly Mexicans, traveling to work the sugar fields. So, he carted himself out of his old comfortable chair and thought, 'Just in case I am asked if I actually paid attention to this warning, I had better get my deputies to check out the buses for a few days.'

CHAPTER 28

Ponchatoula

Hernando picked up me Saturday morning at 9:00am. As of today, my new Mexican name would be, '*Lotcho Futeeno*'. My fake green card, as well as the names of my family, carried the Futeeno name. At first, it had been difficult for the team to learn so many alias names. But they were selected for this mission because they were very smart. Eventually, with much practice their new alias names became second nature and they could recite them without a hitch. Hernando was dropping me off at the bus station. I opened the door to the pickup and tossed my backpack in the truck bed. Hernando, smiled at me from the driver's seat,

"Buenos Dias Lotcho." This was the first time anyone had addressed me with my new Hispanic alias. Quickly I smiled back and responded,

"Buenos Dias, Hernando". We both laughed at my new name.

"I must say, Lotcho; you do look Hispanic in those clothes."

I was wearing an Atlanta Braves ball cap and some old dirty tennis shoes. My white shirt was out over my pants which also appeared old and tattered.

I waved good bye to my team as the truck pulled out onto the sandy road and headed for the highway. It was the first time in

Soft Target
by Larry Greer

over two years that we had been separated. I was still concerned about my men, but was comforted by the fact that they were so well trained.

Hernando reached into his shirt pocket and pulled out a small piece of paper with a phone number and handed it to me,

"This is my number should you, for any reason, need to call me. It is a stolen phone that has been reprogrammed, but once all of you have completed your trip, I will toss it into the river. Of course, as we discussed, you will only be able to call from a pay phone. There are not many pay phones left anymore, but the bus stations always have them. Any issues with using a pay phone?"

"Oh, we practiced using America pay phones when we were in training camp. Trainers asked us many questions in both English and Spanish."

It would soon be June 1st and I wondered how much longer it would be before the real mission would be revealed to me. The truck lumbered along its final leg towards Ponchatoula. I had to admit that I was nervous, but knew it was most important that I not show it. Because it was Saturday, there were a number of pickup trucks loaded with fresh produce, parked in the shade along Main Street. Local women were hovering around the trucks, picking over the produce. Several old men were sitting between clapboard and brick buildings playing checkers in the shade. At a nearby do-it-yourself carwash, teenage boys were cleaning up their cars in preparation for a Saturday night date. I was thinking about how clean and peaceful this little town was. The people appeared relaxed and without fear. There was no open ditch full of stinky sewage running down middle of town. I commented to Hernando on the sweet smell in the air. Hernando told me it was local sugar mill. When the breeze was right you could smell the sugar cane cooking. Hernando interrupted my musings about the local town.

Soft Target
by Larry Greer

"When I get to that traffic light ahead, I will stop and you need to get out and walk to the left. You will see the bus station two blocks down on your right. I recommend you wait till some of the local Mexican farmworkers go into the bus station to get a ticket. Get in line behind them and tell the clerk that you want a one-way ticket to Atlanta. Do not move fast. Watch the Mexicans' mannerisms and copy how they act." He pulled the truck over and stopped,

"Good luck Lotcho and Praise be to Allah."

I looked over at Hernando one last time and shook his hand,

"Allah is with you Hernando, and thank you."

I reached for my backpack and exited the truck, heading toward the bus station. To me, the station had the look of an old gas station. There were benches propped against the outside wall and situated carefully in the shade, under the overhang. A couple of old cars were parked in the street near the entrance. As I approached the station, I saw two Mexicans, sitting on one of the benches near the entrance, deep in conversation. I passed them and looked briefly in their direction, nodding and giving them a slight smile. One of them cut his eyes and quickly nodded his head to the left, motioning inside. When I opened the door I quickly realized his intent. I had not noticed the police car behind the station, but standing at the ticket counter was a police officer who was in a casual conversation with the man behind the counter. I lingered near the entrance and waited for the officer to leave before I approached ticket agent. When the agent looked up at me, the officer also turned back and checked me out. A huge knot developed in my stomach. I knew I had to act as if I had nothing to hide. When I casually stepped up to the counter, the officer moved

Soft Target
by Larry Greer

away but remained within earshot. The ticket agent then asked my destination. In very broken English and with a thick Spanish accent, I responded.

"Atlanta please" The ticket agent responded,
"That will be 49 dollars and 14 cents."

I pulled the worn looking wallet from my pants and found one twenty dollar bill and three tens. The man took it without an issue and punched the ticket to Atlanta. He handed me the ticket and my change. I nodded my thanks and turned slowly towards the officer. I had only taken three steps when the officer spoke.

"Do you speak English?"
"Poco…A little."
"Do you have a green card?"
"Si"

"Show me! He demanded. I pulled my wallet out again and found my forged green card which had been made to look old and worn. I handed it to the officer. His appearance for an officer of the law disappointed me. His uniform needed pressing and he was in need of a shave. He reviewed the green card, turning it over and then asked if he had any other ID. I set my backpack down and opened it up. I found my plastic zip-lock bag and fished out my Mexican driver's license. It showed a recent photo of me and looked very official. The officer stared at it for several minutes, compared it to the green card and asked.

"This license says you are from Acapulco."
"Si, Senior."
"Well what brings you all the way to Ponchatoula?"
"No jobs in Mexico. I come here."
"Why here?" probes the officer.

Soft Target
by Larry Greer

"Sugar farm. I come for job, but no job. I go to Atlanta, and see for restaurant job."

The officer was looking at me closely and asked,

"You Mexican?" I'm getting nervous with this line of questioning.
"My mother si, my father no."
"Where did your father come from?"

Nervously, I looked at the officer straight in the eye and replied,
"Rio, South America."

The officer considered my response and from the look on his face, I figured he believed my story.

"OK, here are your cards." He started to leave and suddenly turned back.
"By the way, you ever been in New Orleans?" I took the cards back and as confidently as I could muster, I replied,

"No sir."

The officer seemed to dismiss me, so I turned and walked outside, and sat near the two Mexicans I had seen earlier. One of them spoke to me in Spanish and asked if the policeman made me nervous?

"Si, a little. Did he ask you questions too?" The closer of the two Mexicans responded.
"He did, but only asked for our green cards. We heard yesterday at the Sugar Mill that there's an alert with local law enforcement. They are looking for Arabs they think came in through New Orleans."

Soft Target
by Larry Greer

I felt a chill go thru my body with this information. I hoped my face did not give me away and decided it best not to get into further conversation with these two. So I inquired if there was a pay phone nearby. They pointed to one on the outside wall. The officer was driving away, so I felt more comfortable calling Hernando, as instructed. I had not expected to use the phone so soon, but the information from the Mexicans and the question from the policeman, were very disturbing. This was no coincidence. Hernando was not expecting a call on this cell phone, so early in my journey.

"Hello," he answered tentatively.
"This is 'S1'. I think we may have a problem."
"What kind of problem?"

"A policeman at the bus station was asking questions about New Orleans and a couple of Mexicans I encountered in front of the bus station said local law enforcement is looking for Arabs that might have made their way into this country through New Orleans."

Hernando found this revelation as alarming as I did and wanted more information about the officer's questions.

"Well he asked me a lot of questions. I did my best to be confident and eventually he seemed o.k. with my documents. Finally he asked me if I had ever been to New Orleans. I told him no. Then when I went back outside, I struck up a conversation with two Mexicans who told me about the alert for Arabs. They had also been questioned and I have this feeling that the police are going to meet every bus that leaves from Ponchatoula. Hernando, I am concerned about my men coming through this route. Perhaps we need to bring two men per bus every day and make sure they travel with Mexicans here in Ponchatoula as I will." Hernando said nothing for a while. He was pondering what would be the safest course of action.

"I have an idea," he finally said. "I will leave earlier with two at a time and drive up to the Sugar Mill where the Mexican farm workers wait for a ride to the bus station. I will offer them a ride and this way your two men can enter the station at the same time as the Mexicans and in that way the officer will not be as suspicious of so many Mexicans coming in from the Sugar Mill together. If there are not any of them waiting at the mill when I go by, we will go back home and wait till the next bus."

This plan sounded good. We agreed that I would call him back tomorrow afternoon from Atlanta to see how things were progressing.

At that moment, the bus roared into the parking lot belching black smoke and kicking up the dust. It loaded all the ticket-holders without much fanfare and soon I was headed towards Atlanta with my two Mexicans acquaintances, and a busload of other Mexicans. Because this bus stopped at every little town along the route, it would take us twelve hours to make it to Atlanta. Now that we were safely on board, I thought it would be good to again talk to the two boys. It might do me good to make their acquaintance, in case I needed their friendship later.

The next morning Hernando picked up two more of the team as planned, and headed directly to the Sugar Mill. As luck would have it, there were four Mexicans waiting under a shade tree for a ride into the Ponchatoula bus station. Hernando slowed the truck, rolled down his window and asked if they wanted a ride to the bus station? One of them replied,

"Si Senior."

Soft Target
by Larry Greer

They eagerly climbed into the back of the pickup with the two S team members. By the time they arrived at the bus station all the men were talking as if they had been friends for years. Hernando knew it was not wise to be seen coming into town with six Mexicans and dropping them off at the bus station. So, he stopped six blocks out of town He indicated he was now about to turn in another direction and they needed to get out. He then took a detour that led him to a street several blocks away. From here, he had a clear view of the bus station. He noticed a police car sitting in the bus station lot. This confirmed Mohamed's information and made him nervous. However, his only other option would be to drive Mohamed's men directly to Atlanta, but that would be very risky. A car loaded with Mexicans was a sure way to get stopped and checked carefully.

Hernando decided to park the truck and walk to a convenience store, where he could see everyone that boarded the bus. He did not have long to wait. The bus arrived on time and after about ten minutes he counted six dark-skinned and two light-skinned men board the bus. As soon as the bus pulled out, the police car took off in another direction. The men had made it.

Soft Target
by Larry Greer

CHAPTER 29

The Journey to Clemson

I sat near the rear of the bus behind the two Mexican boys I had met at the station. As I pondered what might lay ahead for me and my men, I marveled at the freeway. I had never seen roads like this. Large cars and very big trucks sped past us carrying all kind of cargo. I was amazed at America's commerce and the road system that allowed for the flow of goods. The road sides were so clean. In my country trash was tossed everywhere and it was not unusual to see the very poor pick through what lay on the roads, as they searched for food. As we traveled, several times I spotted a police car pulled up behind an old vehicle. More often than not, the occupants of the car looked like Mexicans. They huddled together talking while the policeman searched their belongings. I did not realize the significance of this as we traveled, because I had no understanding of the volume of illegal's crossing into the United States every day. My fear, because of what I had heard, was that they were looking for Middle Easterners. I resolved to call Hernando the next afternoon to make sure the next two team members had gotten on the bus OK.

My bus rumbled through small town after small town. At each stop, they would either pick up passengers or drop them off. Most looked like migrant farmworkers. The frequent stops and the continuous noise from the motor of the bus, made me drowsy. I awoke after several hours of dozing, and dusk was just setting on the little town we had pulled into. The driver announced that we would stop for thirty minutes. If anyone needed to use the restroom or get something to eat, now was the time. One of my two Mexicans acquaintances went by the name of Fernando. He asked if I wanted to join them for a bite. He gestured to a Mexican restaurant across the road. I was hungry, but decided only to go to the restroom. I gave Fernando ten dollars and ask if he would order something for me as well. I told him I was not picky and trusted him to bring back something tasty. Fernando acted happy to do me this favor and took my money. Fifteen minutes later he again boarded the bus and handed me a bag and a drink with my change. Fernando said,

"I got what was quick. I sure don't want the bus to leave without us."

I peered in the bag. An amazing aroma hit my nose and traveled to my empty stomach. I was not quite sure what the food was, but it smelled heavenly and I realized how hungry I was. This was the first truly Mexican food I had ever tasted except for the tortillas back in the river camp. Although the food we had enjoyed in Nicaragua was similar, this Mexican food had different spices. Not too bad! I let Fernando know how grateful I was for befriending me.

We talked for a while and Fernando told me he and his friend were leaving the sugar cane fields, as the harvest was almost over. They were heading to Atlanta to join other migrant workers in the peach orchards just south of Atlanta. Fernando said that he and his buddy had been among the first to leave the sugar fields. Over the next few weeks, there would be many following the same path. It occurred to me that this was going to work well for my team and our plans.

The bus pulled into the Atlanta bus station at 10:25 pm. As I stepped off the bus, I couldn't help but gawk at the many tall buildings, with lights glowing from the windows. So much light,

Soft Target
by Larry Greer

and so many buildings. It was beyond belief. Here in Atlanta, the roads left the ground to rise into the air in a tangle. There were no bicycles or scooters on the roads like I was used to seeing in Pakistan. Neither were there young people walking in large groups. I had never seen so many cars and trucks. Where could they all be going at such a fast speed? As I stood gawking at these new surroundings, my two new acquaintances offered to let me join them at a friend's apartment for the night. I thought about it, but thanked them for their offer and their friendship. I had decided to see if I could get on the next bus to Clemson.

    Like the city, the bus terminal so large; so large in fact that voices echoed off the walls and reverberated through the wide open expanse of brick. Even at this late hour, there must have been over a hundred people milling around, and stretched out on benches despite signs that forbid people sleeping there. Some were sitting in the café drinking coffee, watching TV and eating or reading the newspaper. All this was so new to me, that I decided to sit and just observe my surroundings. I faded into the crowd so I could get my bearings and see where I might find the ticket booth. There were two Policemen deep in conversation in the coffee shop. They appeared not to be concerned about any of the travelers. I caught a glimpse of myself in a nearby kiosk glass and realized that I looked very similar to the many Mexicans in the terminal. I had shaved my long beard before leaving Pakistan six weeks ago and I had not had a haircut since that time either. This was perfect. Many of the Mexicans' hair was worn down over their collars. Evidently they couldn't afford haircuts either. After a few minutes observing, I saw one of the Mexicans get in line at the ticket booth. So I got in line behind him. The Police were still sitting around the corner. This made the timing perfect. My turn at the window and I asked for a ticket to Clemson, South Carolina. The woman behind the window did not even hesitate. In less than a minute I had my ticket. I paid with cash and again took a seat among a group of Mexicans. The bus was scheduled to leave at 12:05am, so I settled

Soft Target
by Larry Greer

in to wait. Because the police were so unconcerned about us, I guessed that there were too many of us for them to check. Just to be sure, I patted my wallet that contained my green card. The bus pulled into the station at 11:55pm. From the looks of how many lined up to board, this would be a full bus. Now the police left their coffee and began walking among those of us in line. They checked green cards of two Mexicans, but did not give me a second glance. I breathed a sigh of relief.

  I boarded the bus and felt the relief of being so close to my final destination. The bus finally pulled out of the station at 12:15am, only 10 minutes late. Our two destinations in South Carolina were Clemson and Greenville. Then the bus went on to Charlotte, North Carolina. As I settled in, I began to worry. Everything to this point had gone so smoothly. I wondered if it had been such a good idea for me to be the first to make the journey. I finally decided it had been the right decision, as I had been able to warn Hernando about the Police. For comfort, I sat next to another dark-skinned man whose country of origin I could not tell. It turned out that the man was a Bolivian. This was not a country I knew. The driver informed the passengers how long each leg of the trip would take. My trip would be four hours to Clemson. That would make it early morning when I arrived. I finally dozed off and must have slept the entire trip, as suddenly I heard the driver announce that Clemson, South Carolina was the next stop. I looked out into the wee hours of morning and could see that there were no tall buildings, as there had been in Atlanta, so I guessed that Clemson was a small town.

  I pulled my backpack down from the overhead rack. It dawned on me that this one bag held all my worldly possessions. Fear crept into my belly as I stepped off the bus and onto the ground at my final destination. I was one of only two people to get off here and the bus quickly pulled away leaving me standing in the deserted parking lot, watching its taillights disappear. The other

Soft Target
by Larry Greer

passenger to step off the bus was a young boy who was also carrying only a backpack. He did not stand there long, as a large, very expensive-looking car pulled up and he was whisked away. I had heard enough about this town and its college, that I assumed he must be a student returning for summer school. I found the doors to the bus station open and ventured inside to the restroom. After relieving myself from the long journey, I looked for the payphone. I found one near the front door. I sat my pack down and put four quarters into the slots on the phone. As directed, I had memorized the number. After three short rings, the call was answered. The voice on the other end sounded like a pre-programmed computer voice,
"The address is 1491 Pendleton Highway." That was the end of the message. The phone went dead and the call disconnected. I focused on memorizing the message. As instructed for safety, I reversed the street number. Other than a few dim street lights, it was still dark. Dawn had not yet shown itself on the Eastern horizon. One block down the street, I spied a yellow cab parked at the corner of a parking lot. Staying out of the glare of the streetlights, I made my way down the block. The cab driver had fallen asleep. I carefully tapped on the hood a couple of times and finally the driver stirred. He cautiously rolled down the window a crack and asked if I needed a ride. When I nodded, he asks for address. When I gave him the address, he took a closer look through his dirty cab window.

"Where you from, boy? India or someplace like that?" I smiled and responded with a nod.
"Yes, sir."
"Well, that will be twelve dollars...in advance."

I pulled the cash from my pocket and handed it to him. He unlocked the rear doors from his driver door and I got in. I did not want the driver to get a good look at my face so I pulled my cap down a little. The driver said,

Soft Target
by Larry Greer

"I don't know what's going on at this college, but it sure does attract a lot of Indians. 'Course, Indians are real smart and all that, but there must be schools in India that are just as good for you'all. So, what brought you here? I mean you are Indian right?"

"Well my fathers a Doctor and he said he thinks that this school has a fine medical program."

That seemed to satisfy the driver. He remained quiet for the remainder of the trip. It wasn't far when he asked,

"What's dat house number again?" I realized that I didn't want the driver to remember the house number, so I replied,

"Just let me out at the nineteen hundred block."

"Suit yourself, boy." And the driver pulled to the side of the road and stopped.
I thanked him and quickly stepped out of the cab. It had been a short drive. Given the long travels I had experienced recently, this surprised me. I checked my watch as I slung my backpack over my shoulder. It was a little after 6:00am. Once I saw that the cab was out of sight, I started walking and taking note of house numbers. At last I noticed 1941 on a box that sat close to the highway. I had heard that this was a box where people received personal mail. Back in Jiba, all mail was picked up at the town meeting hall. Of course, it was rare that anyone received mail in Jiba, so that made it easy.

My home in Jiba was three rooms, two were for sleeping and the other was for cooking and eating and a spot in that room for prayers. By comparison, the house at 1941 Pendleton Street looked very large. It had many glass windows and a high roof. All of this was so different than my childhood home in Jiba. The house sat back in the trees and appeared to be on a rather large

Soft Target
by Larry Greer

piece of land. There were no other homes close by. There was another large building that turned out to be a place for cars. There were curtains on the windows. I could not see any light from within and did not know what to expect when I knocked on the door. I glanced around. In the darkness of the early morning, I heard no sounds and saw no other people. I carefully stepped onto the landing of the front door and lightly knocked. Not knowing what to expect, I stood to the side and waited. Only a moment later, the curtain in the window to my right moved slightly. It appeared that someone was inside. Then a faint noise at the door, indicated a lock was being turned, followed by the sound of a chain being removed. The door opened a crack and a voice asks,

"Who is it?" My voice responded in no more than a whisper,
"It's 'S' One'." Suddenly, the door opened wide.
"Mohamed! It is good to see you!"

I was shocked at who had opened the door. It was a moment before I could respond.

Soft Target
by Larry Greer

CHAPTER 30

The Phone Call

Jason Massey had enrolled at Hartwell University in January so that he could get a semester under his belt before the spring football practice began. However, he did not pass up the chance to practice kicking field goals in his spare time. He had received a very generous scholarship and wanted to make sure he would be worthy of it. His father had several grueling talks with him over the summer. The purpose was to impress on him that girls were not be part of the picture for a few years. He must focus on his studies and football to maintain his scholarship. He remembered the visit he and his father had made to Hartwell University in the previous fall. He loved this place immediately and used the opportunity to see as much of the area as the two-day trip would allow. Of course the first place he wanted to see was that famed stadium. He was overwhelmed by its size. He could just imagine it filled with fans…the noise…the sights and sounds. This was the point at which he made his decision…Hartwell University was definitely his school of choice. Construction of a new wing, to be called the West End Stadium, was well underway. Freshmen recruits had been told it would be ready for the first game in the fall. The East field goal was not part of the construction zone, so Jason figured he could use that end for practice.

John was pleased that Jason had decided on Hartwell and he was also pleased with the scholarship offers. Having this decision behind them, made it easier for John to focus on work and the changes that had happened at the Call Center as a result of the high-level GI meeting at the Pentagon.

John's Call Center had been very busy trying to catch all the incoming calls that were suspect and potentially related to al Qaeda activities. Disposable cell phones were becoming al Qaeda's communication choice. The Call Center in Langley could pick them up, but could not identify who was making or receiving the calls.

Early Sunday morning, John received an excited call from Charley. He had manned the Saturday and Saturday night shifts to cover vacation schedules. With the high alert and "unofficial permission to ignore the FISA Court ruling", they couldn't afford to be shorthanded.

"John, I hate to call you this early and on Sunday, but I think that we have hit on a conversation that could confirm what you heard over at the Pentagon two weeks ago." John took a deep breath. This could be what they had been waiting for.
"Spit it out, Charlie!"

"You need to hear this in person. My guys have spent hours over the past two nights pulling out key words and interpreting references made in this conversation. A full report will be on your desk. You need to get in here, now. I'm, heading home for some much-needed rest, but I'll come back. Once you read the report, call me."
"Thanks Charley, I will leave for the office ASAP. By the way how many words were in the conversation?"

"There are three hundred and five words. But John, I must tell you right now; this call was made to a burn phone from a pay phone. And the answer to your next question is, NO. We did not have time to ping the pay phone. We think the call was made in the Ponchatoula, Louisianan area. The way we picked this call up, was through the 'instant illegal call' forwarded to us by the wireless network. One of my best men was watching for activity in the New Orleans area. Once notified, he connected to the call immediately. I think you'll see that this could be a very important discovery."

Soft Target
by Larry Greer

CHAPTER 31

Cement Truck Journey

Jack Harper arrived early at the junkyard in Georgetown that dealt with used trucks. He had committed to this long haul job for his friend Harry. Today he was picking up the old cement truck and bringing it back to Harry's junkyard for tire inspection. Then tomorrow he'd leave for Clemson, South Carolina. It was easy to pick it out among all the other trucks. At first glance, it looked almost new, but on closer inspection John could see that this was just a cheap paint job disguising a truly worn out old cement truck. Someone had given it a very poor coat of patriotism. The bucket was recurring stripes of red, white and blue. That paint job, made the old cement truck stand out from the rest of the "junkers" in this lot. He just didn't understand who in the devil would pay to go to the expense of hauling this piece of crap all the way down to South Carolina? As he surveyed the large junkyard, the owner emerged from his office.

"Hey there"
"Morning'," replied Jack
"You the guy here to take this old cement barrel to South Carolina?"
"Yea, I just hope the tires will make the trip."
"Well, they do look a mite brittle, don't they?"
"Let me asks you something," Jack said. "Who owns this truck, anyway?"

Soft Target
by Larry Greer

"An old black man bought it from me. By durn, then he took it and had it painted and brought it back here. What's weird is that the truck doesn't even run. He hauled the old heap over to the paint shop and then hauled it back. Makes no sense! He came by late yesterday when I was in the office and said he was going to check the truck out. He didn't do much of a check. Only stayed about ten minutes and left. Only thing I can figure is he has a buddy to work on it down there."

Jack didn't care what the story was, as long as he got his money. He stepped up into the cab of the big Peterbuilt wrecker and backed up close to the old cement truck. After about ten minutes he had it hooked up and waved to the junkyard owner and headed down the freeway to Harry's.

CHAPTER 32

Welcome Home

After Mohamed recovered from the shock of seeing who opened the door, he eagerly steps forward to greet his friend.

"Mohamed, it is very good to see you."
"Valdess!" Mohamed exclaimed.
"Yes, it is I" Valdess grinned. "Are you indeed surprised Mohamed?"
"Well yes, I am. I never thought I'd see you again. It is good to see someone from my country."
"Come in." Valdess directed. "We must close the door."

I looked around. The room was furnished with a nondescript table and chairs. Beside it was a long sofa and a small television perched precariously on a rickety cabinet. Furniture such as this still made me uncomfortable. I noted there were no rugs on the floors like at home. The room was dimly lighted because all the drapes had been pulled tight. I decided that this room would look dark even when it was daylight. Finally, I picked up a familiar whiff of tea. Seeing Valdess and the pungent smell of tea from Pakistan brought a lump to my stomach.

"Would you like a cup of tea? I brought it from Pakistan," Valdess offered.
"Oh, that would be wonderful. I have been craving some food from home for many weeks now."

Soft Target
by Larry Greer

"Put your pack down. Take a chair and relax. You have been on a very long journey. We have much to talk about before the others join us here in South Carolina."
Valdess went into the kitchen and returned with a familiar pot of tea and two cups without handles. That aroma took me back to my village of Jiba and thoughts of my family. Valdess poured the tea, and jerked me back to the present by asking about the trip.

"It went very well and without any real troubles. My only frightful time was a Policeman in Louisiana who asked me many questions and wanted to see my papers. I can only hope that the others are as successful in their journey. They are as well trained, as I was." He wanted Valdess to know that he valued the training received at the camp.
"Because of the policeman's questioning, I called Hernando and we made some changes to our plans for the others. I will call Hernando again today and tell him to advise the others to check their Clemson maps and to walk here from the bus station. I feel it is too risky to have so many from our country riding in cabs to this address, within only a few days."

"I did not see a cab drop you off"

"No, I had him drop me off down the street a ways so he would not know the real address."

"That was good, Mohamed. That sharp thinking is why we selected you to be the leader. Mohamed, you must be tired. After you have had your tea and your prayers to Allah, I suggest you rest. When you awake, we can talk."

"I *am* very tired. Thank you Valdess."
"Come. Let me show you a bed."

Soft Target
by Larry Greer

The room was dark and the bed was soft. Mohamed was instantly asleep.

CHAPTER 33

The Report

John Massey arrived at his office a short hour and a half after Charley's call. His commute was usually longer, but the urgency of Charley's call and the light Sunday morning traffic, condensed his travel time. He spotted the brown envelope on the middle of his neatly organized desk. After settling comfortably in his chair and opened the report. He noted that three others in the office also had a copy. The report, that had been prepared by Charley, predicted the strong possibility of an impending terrorist event. This correlated with the suspicion, coming out of the G1 Pentagon meeting, that several illegals entered the United States thru the Port of New Orleans, about two weeks ago. By now, they could be anywhere in the country, John thought. Several facts made it probable that the Southeast was a target area…but where? John pondered the information that New Orleans had been the entry point and that the phone call in this report most likely came from Ponchatoula. John closed his office door so he could absorb the contents of the 'TOP PRITORITY' report. The facts were as Charley knew them;

A – G1 thinks that a mini sub using stealth technology had arrived and departed from the New Orleans port.
B – A bus station payphone in Ponchatoula, Louisiana had been the location to a disposable, burn phone.
C – Someone using the code name of 'S1' had placed the call to parties unknown.

D – The conversation indicated that there was a problem.
E – The call referenced a local policeman at the bus station.
F – The policeman had asked a lot of questions.
G—'S1' commented that his papers appeared to be OK.
H – The policeman questioned if he had ever been to New Orleans. 'SI responded that he had not.
I – There were Mexicans mentioned in the conversation. 'S1 referenced two of them at the bus station.
J – Mexicans told 'S1 that Homeland Security was looking for Arabs.
K –'S1' referenced others arriving after him through the bus station.
L – 'S1' wanted those who followed, to blend in with Mexicans.
M – The voice on other line mentioned picking up Mexicans at a near by Mill.

    John read the full three hundred and five word transcript five times before leaning back in his chair and closing his eyes to think. He knew his next move should be to call Milton at home. But, this was going to quickly develop into a major manhunt, so before calling Milton, and setting the wheels in motion, he wanted to make absolutely sure he had a full grasp of the facts and the proper interpretation.

CHAPTER 34

Lotcho

Mohamed, or Lotcho, as he would now be called, woke up from a four hour nap. Valdess, pointed him to a bathroom and he enjoyed a long hot shower, a luxury that he had not had since their short stay in Caracas. He wandered his way around the large house until he found the kitchen. Valdess was sitting at a small table studying some drawings.

"Good afternoon Mohamed. Guess I need to begin calling you Lotcho," Valdess adds with a smile. "Did you sleep well?"

"Yes, very well. I really needed that rest. For the first time in days, I did not feel that I had to sleep with one eye open and look over my shoulder."

"I have made you something to eat and there is more tea."
"Thank you. I am both hungry and thirsty for your good tea"
"American food is very strange to me." Valdess offered. "I have found that Mexican food is more to my liking."

Once they had finished their lunch, Valdess cleared their plates and sat back down at the table and pouring himself and Lotcho another cup of tea. There was a long silence. Then with a serious face he began.

Soft Target
by Larry Greer

"Lotcho, you trained at the Madrassas for four years and then at our camp for almost two years. You and your teammates learned many things during that time. Between the twelve of you, you became proficient in English as well as Spanish. On your team are electronics and communications experts, computer experts, as well as small arms and explosive experts. The 'S' team is the most highly trained al Qaeda force to ever come out of Pakistan or Afghanistan, since the brotherhood took down the towers in New York. You would have been too young to know this, but before the attack in 2001, there was another attack on those same towers. They were amateurs, Lotcho, compared to your team. I will reveal to you now, the full details and purpose of your mission. You must keep this information only to yourself. I, Valdess, am ben Laden's most trusted confident. You may remember that I was there at the camp from the day you arrived till the day you left with the other eleven members. Did you realize that?" Mohamed had not put that together until this moment. Valdess continued,

"My time there with you, was for one purpose. I had to be positive that you and your team were the right ones to send on this mission. As you know, up to this point the logistics have been flawless. Your mission has been very carefully planned. ben Laden is a mastermind when it comes to this kind of planning. The plan is his! We are the chosen ones who will carry out that plan. Until now, no one who has assisted you along the way knows any of the details about the mission. All were trained and prepared to do their job and only their job." Valdess stopped for emphasis and took a breath, as he looked Lotcho in the eye.

"Lotcho, this is very, much important. You are now only the third person to know the plan in its entirety."

CHAPTER 35

The Mission Revealed

Much goes through my head at this moment. I reached for the teapot and poured myself another cup to calm my nerves. Because I want Valdess to know that he had selected the right person to lead our team, I am hoping that my nervousness does not show. He had intimidated me greatly while I was at the camp. We all had a healthy respect for him. Now he is sitting at this table and talking with me almost as an equal. I sensed this was an important turning point in our mission, for several reasons.

Valdess continued,
"Lotcho, once I have given you all the details of the entire plan, I will leave you. I am returning home tomorrow. My visa is expiring and I must return to Pakistan. I came into this country, assisting a diplomat, but if I do not leave America soon it will be dangerous for your mission. I do not want to create any suspicion about Pakistan's involvement, when your mission is complete. You must know the official Government of Pakistan is not directly involved. We do not want them implicated in any way. I have been in Clemson for almost three weeks. Your rent and other expenses of the house have been paid up for six months. Your cover with the landlord is that you are all students.

Valdess noticed that Lotcho's hands could not be still. The nervousness was obvious and accompanied by a tightening of the jaw. This was good. He knew Lotcho was taking his mission and this information seriously.

"Mohamed, are you OK?" Valdess used his real name to garner attention. He wanted an honest answer.

"Yes, Valdess, I am fine, but I must admit that after such a long time of anticipation, I am nervous. I regret that it shows."

"I am not surprised and just so you know; I would be the same in your shoes. I would have expected this reaction."

After a long pause, Valdess continued,
"Alright, listen closely. On November 30th of this year, there is a very traditional football game at the University stadium. This stadium holds eighty-four thousand people. I can guarantee you that on this day, it will be not only full, but over-flowing. You and your team will be in that stadium. Your mission is to take all the people in that stadium hostage."

"What!" I had not expected anything like this. My head was spinning. It dawned on me that Valdess had gone mad.

"How is that possible? We are, but twelve men!"
"Silence," he interrupted sharply. "Leading up to this date, many other things will transpire. Let me tell you all the details.

"I will give you the phone number of a man that specializes in getting many of his people jobs. Most of them have come to this area illegally from Mexico. He receives a small sum for this service as long as the men maintain their jobs. You must contact him after all of your team arrives. Tell him you need work for your men. Tell him your men are expert as grounds keepers and on construction sites. He will most likely place you at the University. There are jobs for landscaping, lawn maintenance and painting. It will be important for some to get work on the construction site of the stadium. This will put you in a position to study the stadium layout far in advance of the mission. There are only eight main gates where the people enter or exit. The East End gate under the score board is used only for the players at the beginning of the game. These gates are closed before and after the players have entered and no one else is allowed in or out of this entrance. Six of your men will be assigned to cover the six primary gates and no one will be allowed leave the stadium. You will all have the very latest technology devices to communicate with each other. Security of the gates will occur after you have taken the players hostage. This action will obviously take the crowd by surprise. We believe they will initially think it is a publicity stunt."

I am shocked by Valdess' words. How on earth are 12 men going to capture an entire team, much less 84,000 spectators?

"May I ask a question or two as we go?"
"Please do. I will need to get my breath, periodically."

"I have watched American football. There are maybe 50 players! How are we, as only 12 men, to capture them? Several of the games I watched on ESPN when we were in the camp, were football games. These players were running all over the field before the game! I've seen that!"

"You must believe that this plan is flawless. It has been very well thought out. It will be flawless, if you execute it flawlessly. Remember that I too have watched the game of football, Lotcho." Valdess retorted.

"I have very carefully studied this team and their stadium. You and your team will attend many games before this last game when you complete your mission. In that way you will have plenty of opportunity to study the players and how they enter the stadium.

Soft Target
by Larry Greer

You will also have many opportunities to observe the crowd's behavior. I can tell you, it is very predictable! What you will discover is that before the game starts, the Hartwell Team boards three buses and drives from the lower level of the West End of the stadium around to the North stands. They then stop at the end of the East End gate. That gate opens up just long enough for the players to get off the buses. At this time, a canon shoots off a loud explosive. At that sound, the crowd rises to their feet and makes tremendous noise. Many musicians will be playing while the football players run under the score board, down the hill and onto the playing field. You will see this tradition repeated at each game. You must memorize every aspect of this tradition!"

My head is still spinning, and I ask,
"But still, how do we round them up? Once our intentions are clear, will they not take the opportunity to run in all directions as they do doing an actual game?"

"Ah, that is an excellent question. Here is the plan. When the players board their buses, three of the 'S' team, including yourself, will each board a bus. You will have a mask along with a weapon. You must board very last on each bus. Once the players see you and your gun they will freeze. In a normal voice, you will instruct them to keep their seats so no harm will come to them. Of course, they will not believe you, but they will remain quiet. Remember, these men are well, trained in their football. They are leaders, just as you are. You must watch for any who try to be heroes in this situation. Do not allow them to disrupt your mission. If that happens, fire one shot in the roof and level your gun directly at him. The plan calls for you to order the driver to head off in the planned route. The other two busses will follow. When you get near the East gate, you tell the driver to take a wide swing and rather than stopping to let the boys out, he must turn right and jump the curb. You will instruct him to drive under the score board and directly down the hill. Direct him to blow his horn to warn those who might be standing along the hill to clear out of the way. The next two buses will be given the same instructions by the 'S' team member on board and they will follow the first bus. The crowd will think all this is a spectacular stunt and will not know what to think. Once the three buses are in the middle of the field one behind the other, instruct the bus driver to stop. You will turn on your remote mike and your communication expert and another member of your team will have stepped into the communication command center which is above the South seats. They will lock everyone inside. Once the communications expert is in the room and at the controls he will be able to patch you into the main sound system. This will allow you to address everyone in the stadium. Your video expert will take over the center that controls the score board and can project live action pictures on the big screen. He will direct the cameraman to zero in on the first bus which will be the one that you are in. At this point, you will be live on the sound and video systems. The crowd will see the lead bus on the big screen and will know where your voice is coming from. You calmly instruct the crowd to remain calm, remain in their seats and no harm will come to them. Be very clear in letting them know that you are serious. At this point, there will be some who feel that they can get out. This is when your other six team members are to stand at the six gates with their guns pointed. They are to let any spectators know that they will be shot if they approach the gate. By this time, all your team members will have stripped off their top layer of clothing and all will be in black shirts and pants. With their black mask, there will be no mistaking them. They must make it clear that their intent is to shoot to kill,

      All I could manage was to shake my head in disbelief.
"What is it?" ask Valdess, with disappointment and disgust in his voice.

      "I just never dreamed…" and my voice tailed off, as I couldn't even finish the sentence. I cannot get my head around

Soft Target
by Larry Greer

this plan. I am trying to imagine how we would think my group of 12 men could control over eighty thousand people. Is that even possible? Finally, I managed to continue,

"There is going to be mass hysteria."

"We have reason to believe that you are right. You must gain control by your threats. If that does not work, you will give them one example of what will happen to them if they got out of hand."

"What kind of warning will that be?" I ask in trepidation.

"The morning of the game one of your team will steal a West End parking pass out of a car that is already in its parking spot. You will have acquired a small pick-up truck with a University sticker on the doors. There will be four large ice chests in the bed of the truck. These chests will contain four hundred pounds of TNT. With this official-looking truck, the driver will be able to take it past the police and find an inconspicuous spot to park the truck. If a warning needs to be sent to the crowd, you will blow up the truck. This will be done by remote control. The explosion will shock the crowd and should keep them in their seats. You will tell them that there are more explosives like this hidden under the stands where they sit and that you will not hesitate to set these off."

Suddenly, I understood how the warning would work. It would become clear to every spectator that excessive amounts of explosives were hidden under the stands. If they bolted or did not do as instructed, the result would be complete disaster. At that moment, I believed the plan, although outrageous, might just work. Perhaps I could control a crowd of 84,000 people. However, if there was a glitch in this plan, I had a feeling it would be with the communications.

Soft Target
by Larry Greer

Valdess stood and without a word, headed outside. Although he said nothing, I knew it was to have a cigarette. This ban on smoking inside was foreign to us. In Pakistan, people smoked everywhere. I was relieved to have some time to digest the details of this unbelievable plan. I knew Valdess would be continuing his instructions when he returned. As I rested my head on my arms, I prayed he would take his time.

CHAPTER 36

The Delivery

The old Peterbilt wrecker left Georgetown bright and early on Monday morning and headed south on I-95. The powerful truck pumped out a cloud of dirty black smoke, but had no trouble pulling its heavy load over the mountain passes. At the crest of the mountain, Jack Harper could see that the downhill grade was quite severe. He delighted in punching the Jake brakes, causing the dual chrome-plated exhaust pipes to reverberate a back draft. This long-haul trip was a treat for Jack. Retirement had not been all he had anticipated and he had missed the smell of diesel, the camaraderie with other truckers and the freedom of the open road. He was relieved that the old cement truck was making the trip without incident. He wondered more than once, why anyone would pay the hefty price to have this dilapidated old truck hauled all the way to South Carolina. It just did not make sense. However, because he was being handsomely paid for this crazy job, he kept that concern to himself.

As the sun fell below the horizon, he realized he had been on the road over 12 hours and decided to find a cheap motel and get some shut-eye. As he approached the first exit for Charlotte, North Carolina, he noticed a police road check in the north-bound lanes of Interstate 85. Jack was glad he was in the South-bound lane, as he knew the trucks involved in that check could be held up for hours. All he wanted was some hot food and a bed.

Soft Target
by Larry Greer

Jack pulled into a 24-hour truck stop and plopped down in a booth. There appeared to be only one waitress in the place and she looked as if she had been on duty way too long. When she finally noticed him, she came over to his booth and just stood there with pen and pad in hand. In an attempt to be friendly, Jack asked about the roadblock. With a disinterested response she said it had something to do with checking licenses, but most of the truckers thought they were really looking for illegals. Wearily, she added that this nonsense had been going on for 3 days.

A trucker in the next booth piped up,

"Man, I've never seen a road check like this before. They even have the exits blocked three miles up the road so we couldn't pull off even if we were warned about the roadblock. The cops go at it for hours…backs the traffic up for miles. Damnedest thing I ever saw."

Jack responded to the trucker,
"Wow, I did long-haul for years and never ran into a check like that before."

CHAPTER 37

U.S. Intelligence

Two hours after John Massey absorbed Charley's report, he was sitting on Milton's patio with a cup of coffee, watching Milton as read the report. He put the report down on the wicker table and looked as if he were about to speak. Then he picked up the report again and re-read it. John was not surprised, as he had read it twice again before heading for Milton's house. After the second reading, Milton threw the paper down on the table again, and slammed his hand down on the document,

"Damn John, this is significant. It all adds up: the concern of the sub Captain and the phone call from this unknown 'S1'. These can't be unrelated. What has me really concerned is that the phone call Charley intercepted was yesterday. Some of these people could be five hundred miles inland by now, and it sounds like there could be more following." Milton sprang into action. He stood and headed into the house. "I'm going to call a meeting. You get Homeland Security and the FBI up to speed and meet me at headquarters in 30 minutes."

There would be no communication gaps this time. Milton brought all the agencies together and filled them in. As a result, the FBI was all over the Ponchatoula bus station within hours. A very frightened ticket agent pleaded that it was normal for Mexicans to catch a bus here. He did not think there was anything unusual about the passengers the last few days. He told the agents that the local mill hired a lot of them during the sugar cane harvest, but the

harvest was almost over, so the pattern of farm workers was to move on to the peach orchards in Georgia and South Carolina.
"I know the sheriff's deputies have been around here a little more than normal, but I thought they were just after the drugs. They don't tell me 'nuthin'. You go talk to them."
The FBI agents had not learned much from the ticket agent, but took him up on his suggestion to check out the sheriff's office.

"Well," pondered Sheriff Dilworth. "We see a lot of Mexicans through here about this time of year. Come to think about it, there were a number of them that seemed a little smarter than the rest. I didn't think too much 'bout it at the time. Just figured we were gettin' more of the educated Mexicans since their economy is getting worse."

The lead FBI agent, Marc Wilson picked up on the Sheriff's comment.
"What do you mean they were smarter? What made you think that?"

"Well, I mean, they looked me straight in the eye and didn't hesitate with their answers. Usually these illegals can't speak no English and they're intimidated by the police. They won't even look you in the eye when you're talkin' to 'em. Those smart ones, they were really sure of themselves. And they didn' seem to have a problem understandin' English. They spoke pretty good too, for farm workers just comin' into this country. That's why I thought they seemed more educated."

"How many have you talked to that met this description?"
"Oh, I would say six or seven."

"How many Mexicans or other foreign-looking people have gone through the bus station since you received word to be on the lookout?"

Soft Target
by Larry Greer

"Oh, maybe fifty or sixty; I mean we don't do no written report or head count if you know what I mean."

"Sheriff, did you get a copy of the Homeland Security mug shots of the Nine Eleven men?"

"Ya, sure, but you know, they all look alike to us. 'Sides, legally, we can't haul their asses in and interrogate 'em real close. You Feds tie our hands on that stuff! Your Immigration boys do that job."

"OK Sheriff, we appreciate your time. Here is my number. You call me if you see ANYTHING suspicious in the next few weeks." The FBI agents headed out and Agent Marc Wilson sent a report back to the FBI office and Homeland Security.

Back at Langley, the decision had been made by Homeland Security to conduct eighteen interstate road checks to see what they might find. Office of Immigration was included in case they needed to pull any illegals in for further questioning. An orange alert was sent to all airports and bus stations on the entire East Coast. The warning alerted officials to profile for anyone with an Arab appearance trying to pass themselves off as Mexicans.

For John Massey, this meant his Call Center would be on high alert. He informed his staff that FISA was possibly being rolled back. They were to pull out all the stops. He would personally take any heat from Congress. He emphasized that particular attention needed to be paid to the Ponchatoula, Louisiana area and northward to Atlanta. Also, they were to immediately notify to him if they heard any reference to the term "S1".

CHAPTER 38

The Master Plan

Lotcho was still sitting in the kitchen when Valdess came back in from his smoke break. He was becoming cognizant that his carefree childhood had been short. Even at a young age, he had assumed responsibility for his father's herd. Then the past two years of training at the camp in Pakistan, had matured him way beyond his 21 years and infused a hatred for the Western world and for all that white people represented. Although Valdese's plan was frightening, he realized he wanted the satisfaction of destroying that stadium and all in attendance. This was his mission. Allah would be pleased. His fear was eased by that thought.

Valdess took the teapot from the stove and offered Lotcho another cup. Lotcho motioned that he did not care for more.

"I have had time to consider your plan. I believe I understand. But I do have a few questions." Lotcho said.

"If I am to take these football players hostage, what am I asking for in return for their release?"

Valdess took another sip of his tea. For emphasis, he placed the cup down slowly, before speaking.

"Lotcho, this is the genius of our leader, bin Laden. When your man in the communications booth has your face on the

Soft Target
by Larry Greer

jumbotron screen, for all to see, and the sound system is projecting your voice to all in the stadium, our communications expert will then link you into the stadium's Homeland Security hot line. Because of our success in 2001, all locations where crowds gather are now connected to the American Government's Homeland Security hot line. These lines are carefully monitored. When you make yourself known, all forces of the military and all security agencies in the United States will tune into Hartwell Stadium. It will only be minutes before the President of the United States will be alerted to this hostage situation. You, Lotcho, will announce that you wish to speak to the President himself. You will announce to everyone in the stadium that their safety is in President's hands.

"How do you know for a fact, that there is a hot line in the Stadium's communications directly to Homeland Security?"

"It is time for you to understand more, Lotcho. For several years now, we have had two moles planted deep in Homeland Security. They are our eyes and ears into the United States security networks. What I am now telling you will work."

"Valdess, my concern is in the communications room. How do we make sure our man is familiar with the operations and confident that he can make the right connections to Homeland Security?"

"You must find a way to get your man hired as a technician before the big game. The other communications staff must feel that he belongs there, so as not to arouse suspicion. I also suggest that you and your team attend all Hartwell football games. You will become familiar with the workings of the stadium and the personnel who run the events. On the day of your mission, your man in the communications booth will have a gun at the lead technician's head. That will make sure you get into Homeland Security."

"May I ask again, what is the amount of the ransom?"

"I did not say there was an amount. Money is not what this is about."

"Oh. Then what is our mission, Valdez?"

"You are familiar with Guantanamo, Cuba where the Americans are keeping about two hundred and seventy of our brother's captive?"

"Yes, I have heard of the evils perpetrated on our brothers in that hell-hole!"

"Our purpose in this very important mission is to secure the release of our brothers in exchange for the lives of 84,000 Americans in the Hartwell Stadium. Your demand of the President of the United States is to immediately release our brothers to the authorities of the Cuban Government. We have developed strong bonds with the Castro regime in Cuba and have secured their promise to deliver our brothers back to us. They will be boarded on a Russian ship that is delivering goods to Cuba. In return, al-Qaeda has agreed to assist Cuba when it needs help against the Americans."

My thoughts were swirling: *This is truly a master plan and I, Mohamed from the little village of Jiba, am to lead this jihad for my brothers.* While Valdess smoked I had absorbed, what I thought was the majority of the plan. I am now realizing that there is much, much more for me to learn.

"But what if the President will not meet my demand?"

"He will of course be bluffing, and will await your response. The Americans value the lives of individual people too much. He would not jeopardize their lives in fear of how the American public would react.

Soft Target
by Larry Greer

"Lotcho, you must be prepared to demonstrate the seriousness of your intentions, and communicate that to the President. If necessary, you must send a message to all those in the stadium and to the American Government that you are very willing to blow up all 84,000 people if they do not meet your demands. The President and his advisors will want to know what you are prepared to do next. At this time, you will hold a remote control that will detonate the dynamite that has been placed in the truck. You will then tell him that the entire stadium is wired with explosives and should he not meet your demands, you and your team will are prepared to become martyrs for Allah and eighty thousand American infidels will all die."

It was becoming clear to me that this very intricate plan had been in the works for many years. I truly appreciated the brilliance of our leader Osama bin Laden.

"Valdess, tomorrow, my team will begin to show up here prepared to carry out our mission. What do you suggest I share with them of this plan?"

"Give them a couple of days to recuperate and become accustomed to their new surroundings. Keep them in and around the house for now. In a week, bring them together as a group. They were selected for this mission because they are trustworthy and dedicated to Allah's plan. Share what you feel comfortable sharing at this time, but for safety, do not share all the details."

"How will we know the mission has been successful? Who will let us know that the men at Guantanamo have been freed?"

"This is where the American media will be useful to you. Have the men in the communications booth split the big screen, so you can watch CNN. It will not take long for the world-wide media to get news of your actions. There will also be another benefit of displaying CNN on the Hartwell jumbo-tron. All 84,000 hostages will see that this is real and your control over them will become stronger. We have also asked the Cuban media to televise the gate at Guantanamo watching to see if the prisoners are released. This too, will be picked up world-wide. The Cuban army is prepared to take charge of the prisoners as they leave Guantanamo."

    I continued to be amazed at the detailed nature of this plan. I also became aware that there were no plans for our escape at the end of this journey. With great difficulty, I willed my mind to focus on my mission for my brethren and for Allah.

CHAPTER 39

Ponchatoula Camp

Raga and Johey were to be the last of the team to leave their camp in the swamps of Ponchatoula. Hernando found them packed and anxious to leave. It had been raining throughout the night and cloak of humidity enveloped everything. Even the bed of Hernando's truck held several inches of water. As Hernando's truck lumbered down the muddy road, it was impossible to avoid large ruts filled with rainwater. If Raga and Johey were not already soaked, now they were also covered in mud. The river, along which they had camped, was rising and if they had waited much longer, departure might have been impossible.

Hernando slowed to cross a stream that had been created by the heavy rains. He leaned out his window to tell the men,

"I cannot take you the same route as the others. There is a problem at the Ponchatoula bus station. We have heard rumors that Federal agents are looking for Arabs passing themselves off as Mexicans. You must be exceedingly careful on your journey."

Raga, who was a worrier by nature, was concerned.

"What are we going to do? Did the others going before us run into trouble? Has anyone been detained? How are we going to get to Atlanta without going through Ponchatoula?" His questions seemed endless to Hernando.

"Patience, Raga. Yes, your brothers have made it through to Clemson without raising suspicion. No one has been arrested or detained. I have given a great deal of thought to an alternate route. I will drive you to Branson, Missouri and put you on the bus there. In this way you will bypass Atlanta and go to Ashville, North Carolina. If anyone is looking for Arabs coming into Atlanta on the bus, they will not find you. From Asheville, you will connect with a bus to Greenville, South Carolina. This is an entirely different route and you will be safer."

Johey then asked, "Why are you taking us through Branson."

"Branson is a big tourist town. Many Mexicans are hired to work in their restaurants and hotels. No one will take a second look at Mexicans getting on or off a bus in that town. Here, however, is my caution. When you get off the bus in Greenville, South Carolina, you must fine and hire a Mexican to drive you to Clemson. Do not get on the bus going to Clemson, as the police or even federal officials may be watching that bus station. Once you get into Clemson, ask your driver to look for the location of a pay phone. There are not many anymore. Try to avoid the one at the bus station. Your driver, who will be familiar with illegal Mexicans wanting to avoid the Immigration police, will understand if you refuse to call when you see police at the station. Make your phone call and get the address to where the rest of your team is waiting for you. Do not let the Mexican take you to the address. Give him the name of the street only. Then get out and walk rest of the way."

The alternate route and detailed instructions made Raga and Johey feel more comfortable. They settled back on their wet packs, prepared for the 10-hour ride to Branson. Hernando let them out a block from the bus station and said his final good-byes. His part of the mission was now complete.

CHAPTER 40

The Agencies

Joseph Black had served as the Asst. Director of the FBI since the new President had come into office almost eight years ago. His primary responsibility, early on, had been to develop the new Homeland Security Department. Not only was Joseph Black politically savvy, but he had many years of experience developing organizational structure within the government. He was well aware that bureaucrats thrived on taking credit for success, even if they had nothing to do with it. He was adept at making department heads feel important and in-the-know. Joseph had been one of the first on Milton's list for the 'G1' meeting the weekend before. The two men had risen to the top of their respective organizations.-- Milton at the CIA and Joseph at the FBI. The two men had developed a healthy respect for each other and worked together well.

When it came to the threat of al-Qaeda operatives in the United States, both the FBI and the CIA had learned how important it was to cooperate. Unfortunately *Nine-Eleven* had taught them that competition between the two agencies was not an effective tool in the fight against al-Qaeda. Both men's primary concern today was locating and uncovering any cell activity before it could be executed.

"Joe" and "Milt" as they called each other were the two that had developed the initial plan of attack. Collaboration with the Department of Immigration and surveillance around all modes of transportation had been Joe's responsibility. Phone surveillance and law enforcement notification had become Milt's tasks. John Massey's Call Center no longer had surveillance restrictions. They were highly focused on any call referencing someone known as "S1".

When the first round of questioning revealed nothing useful, Joe and Milt agreed to circle back to the first point of contact in Ponchatoula at the sugar mill and at the bus station. Then the Atlanta bus station was revisited with different agents, to make sure nothing had been overlooked. Both Joe and Milt were copied on all communication. Neither wanted a repeat of what happened before the *Nine-Eleven* tragedy.
Joe cringed every time he remembered the FBI agent who tried in vain to bring attention to the number of Arabs taking flight instruction in this country. Unfortunately for hundreds of Americans in the New York Towers, that agent's report never got the attention it deserved.

Several days into the investigation, Joe thought they might have uncovered something important. As a result of the second trip to the Atlanta bus station, one of his agents discovered that ten tickets purchased on sequential days, contained the exact same route from Ponchatoula to Clemson, South Carolina. Joe set up a call between himself, Milt and the agent who made the report. He wanted to hear it firsthand.

"Sam, this is Joe Black in Langley. I have Director Milton West from the CIA on the phone with us."

"Good afternoon Director Black, Director West," came Sam's slightly nervous response. He had never met Joseph Black or spoken to him on the phone. These men were many levels above his pay grade.

"Sam, I just received a copy of your report about the Atlanta bus tickets. How did this information come to your attention? I didn't know anyone kept records on the ethnicity of ticket purchasers."

"Ah, Director Black--- it is unofficial, but the Immigration Dept. has asked certain bus stations to keep an informal record of how many Hispanics are traveling up the northern corridor. They wanted to keep informed about the potential of illegals moving from the Southwest or Florida. So when we checked their tickets, we were able to confirm that ten Mexicans had come thru the Atlanta bus station in the past week with Clemson as their final destination."

"Did they divulge how they kept these records?"

"Director, as I said it is unofficial and very low tech. A check mark is made on the corner of each stub, indicating the ethnic background of the traveler. Those stubs go into a file marked for the Clemson station."

"Thank you Sam. Your keen observation skills have been very helpful."

In order to maintain the line of command, Joe immediately called Sam's boss to let him know he had talked to Sam directly and reported on his good work.

The next step was to check this information with the ticket agent at the Clemson bus station. Unfortunately, the ticket agents were not helpful. The only information they could share was about the large number of East Indian students going back and forth to Atlanta. Joe wasn't sure this was relevant, but added it to his file.

Soft Target
by Larry Greer

After discussion with Milt, Joe contacted Immigration and suggested they place a few plain clothes agents at the Clemson bus station to watch for anything unusual.

Soft Target
by Larry Greer

CHAPTER 41

Mecca

At the time Mohammad had arrived in Clemson, South Carolina, his Mother and Father along with his younger brother Hasped, who was now fifteen years old, embarked on an once-in-a-lifetime journey. Monfar, Mohamed's father, was now approaching sixty years old and he did not think he could wait much longer to make the twenty two hundred mile pilgrimage from Islamabad to Mecca that was on the far side of Saudi Arabia. For years he had put aside money for this long trip. He knew that taking Hasped along would add to his expense, but he wanted Hasped to experience Mecca. He also needed his help carrying baggage. Monfar was not a young 60 and years herding sheep had taken its toll on his strength and stamina. The next pilgrimage would begin the last week of November in 2008, so they would need to begin their trip around the first of November. Monfar had been smart enough to contact a travel agent in the city of Texila to help with the plans and secure places to stay along the way. This he had done one year ago. The trip would be made partially by bus and partially by boat. There would be thousands of others also making the same trip and this worried Monfar.

A month before they were to leave they had a visitor. He introduced himself as Valdess, a friend of their son Mohamed. Valdess told them that he would be seeing Mohamed sometime in the future and he would pass along any message that they might want to get to their son. Monfar knew enough not to ask where their son was, but said to tell Mohamed he is missed and especially by the sheep. He smiled when he said it and Valdess understood it to be only his attempt at humor. Monfar's wife asked if Valdess would take a recent photo of the three of them to Mohamed. Valdess said he would be happy to do it. When Monfar told Valdess about their plans to go to Mecca, Valdess volunteered to give him an official looking paper with his name on it and told Monfar to show it at the bus stations or hotels and the ship master. Along the way and he should get much better treatment. There was no proof, but rumors had it that Valdess was a top ranking bin Laden henchman and he was treated with the utmost respect.

Soft Target
by Larry Greer

CHAPTER 42

Valdess's Departure

I did not sleep well that night after learning of the master plan. The mission as laid out by Valdess weighted heavily on my mind. Valdess had said he would be leaving to start his trip back to Pakistan in the morning and this meant that I would be left alone to carry out the plan of a man that had not been seen in public since before the nine eleven attack. I turned and tossed most of the night and thinking about my life and what would become of me. Many young men my age had given their lives in recent years.
I understood the master plan for getting the prisoners released in Cuba but nothing had been said about what would happen to the 'S' Team. In the darkness of my room, I now allowed myself to ponder the possibilities. The only plausible conclusion was death or an American prison for the remainder of our lives. I felt both honor and fear at the unfolding of this mission that I had committed, I realized I had been selected for a very special honor among Muslims. I for the first time since I had left Pakistan I got down on the floor in my bedroom and faced Mecca at the appointed time of prayer and thanked Allah.

The next morning I met Valdess in the kitchen. I almost did not recognize him. He had on American-style clothing. His face was clean-shaven and he had exchanged his turban for a ball-cap. I sneaked peaks at him all during our breakfast of bread and tea. Feeling that this was an important moment between us, I ask him if he would join me in prayer. After our prayers, he took me back to the kitchen chairs and said he wanted to tell me a few things before he left this morning.

"Before I left Pakistan on my last visit, I went by your village of Jiba and spoke to your mother and father. Your father said to tell you that they missed you very much and especially did the sheep." This brought a smile to my normally serious face.

"Your mother gave me this photo. It was of a much older couple than I remembered and a much more mature Hasped. I clutched it to my chest.

"Your father wanted you to know that he has long been saving for a pilgrimage to Mecca. They will in mid-November, to join the December gathering of pilgrims. As you know, it's over 3,500 miles. This will be a difficult journey, as he is not a well man, but Hasped will be a big help. I gave them a personal letter of commendation. It will help your father get the best seats on the bus and good rooms at the hotels. I also gave your father the money that was promised to your family when you committed to this mission. It is more than what you would have earned for the family if you had been herding sheep at home. Mohamed, now, I must say goodbye."

I noted that he with a soft voice used my real name. Valdess picked up his backpack, flung it over his shoulder, and put both his hands on my shoulders. In the custom of our people, he kissed me on both cheeks and said in parting,
"Remember, Allah is great and Allah goes with you on your sacred mission."

With that, Valdess went out of the door of the American house and headed towards town. I watched his back until I could no longer see him. My heart was heavy as I knew this would be the last time I would ever see my friend and mentor Valdess.

CHAPTER 43

Raga and Johey's Journey

As Raga and Johey were changing buses in Ashville, North Carolina, the other nine team members, who had arrived in Clemson without incident, were entertaining each other with tales of their individual journeys from Ponchatoula. They were happy to again be among brethren. However, Mohamed who now used his alias Lotcho was not happy. Raga and Johey, for some reason had not yet joined them and he worried. On the second day after they should have arrived, Lotcho gave serious thought about using the phone that Hernando had given him for emergencies. He could not bring himself to do this for he feared the American government network might pick up his call and trace it back to Clemson, so he continued to worry.

On the morning of the third day, there was a knock on the door. When Lotcho opened it, there stood a grinning Raga and Johey. Everyone was relieved to see them and was eager to hear the story of their journey to Clemson. They talked about the trip in Hernando's muddy truck to Branson, the trip from Asheville to Greenville and the Mexican that had given them a ride from Greenville to Clemson for only $50. Lotcho knitted his brows and Raga, observing the change in expression, assured Lotcho that they had been dropped off several miles down the road. He shared the local gossip about Immigration authorities who were supposedly looking for Middle Easterners, posing as Mexicans. The Mexican driver took only one look at their faces and after that, he never looked them in the eyes again. This behavior made Raja concerned that the Mexican was suspicious about them. He told the others that it was a relief when they had been dropped off and could walk the last mile.

After several days, Lotcho heard all their travel stories. He gave the men several weeks to settle into their new environment. At the beginning of week three, Lotcho felt it was time to share more of the mission with the men, so he asked all of them to join him in the main living quarters.

"We have all heard the rumors about the immigration and customs men looking carefully in this area. This American intelligence group is known as ICE. That stands for Immigration and Customs Enforcement. I have no idea who they are looking for or if they are onto our mission. We know they are not sure of our numbers, but have suspicions that there are several of us. If we lay low for two more weeks and give them nothing to observe, I believe they will cool down and look at other locations.
"Now, it is time for me to share more about our mission. First, let me tell you that tomorrow I will make contact with a man that will find jobs for us. He makes connections for many immigrants looking for work. He never asks questions, but a little deception will give us more protection. I will tell him that a 'Coyote' is bringing in eleven illegals from Texas in two weeks and that I would like for him to find jobs for them. He will be told that some of you have electrical experience. This means you could assist with electrical projects. Some of you will fit the skills for general construction work. I will inquire about the new Hartwell West End Stadium presently under construction. Because I need to remain flexible, I will not take a job at this point. You will need to make sure you have your Green Cards. That is all you will need to get the type of job we need you to have for the mission. Now about the mission…"

Soft Target
by Larry Greer

For the next two hours Lotcho covered the plans and allowed for questions as he went along. He was not surprised by the incredulous look on the men's faces. He had been just as stunned the first time Valdess shared the plan with him. They too, had guessed wrong about the mission and what would be expected of them. The *nine eleven group* had taken over three thousand Americans with them to their deaths in order to bring a message to the infidels. That message had not changed. People of Islam still wanted the Americans out of the Middle East and they were willing to make personal sacrifices, including death, to make their point. Now as he shared the details with his men, they began to realize that this mission could possibly mean death for tens of thousands or it could mean freedom for two hundred and seventy prisoners in Cuba.

Soft Target
by Larry Greer

CHAPTER 44

The Search

Joe Black felt the FBI and CIA investigation he had undertaken with Milt had come to a standstill. He listened over and over to the recorded tape of the "S1' voice. Then he read and reread the report that highlighted the recorded conversation. Neither the recording, the report nor the interviews he had with men in the field, revealed clues as to why these men had come into the United States by a submarine as opposed to the almost opened border between America and Mexico? He had a gut feeling there were a number of them, but no proof to that effect. Information revealed from the Atlanta and Ponchatoula bus station employees indicated that they ended up somewhere near Clemson, South Carolina. But none of this made any sense. If they did end up in Clemson, what could be their possible objective?

It had now been two weeks since the 'S1' phone tap and all leads had come to a dead end. The phone lines were silent. Where were these people? There were sixteen undercover agents working the Clemson area, but none of them had come up with the slightest evidence that Middle Easterners were in the area. The students had gone home for the summer and the town felt nearly deserted. A few summer school students created the only activity. Even the bars were sparse, as locals headed to Lake Hartwell for the hot summer months. None of the agents reported anything unusual.

Soft Target
by Larry Greer

Joe was now convinced that if they had ever been in Clemson they were now on their way somewhere else. However, he couldn't shake the question about why they came to Clemson in the first place. It nagged at him constantly. Several of the investigation team thought maybe Clemson had been chosen because it was a small community tucked in the hills of a rural Southern state, others speculated that it was simply a diversion and some suggested it was a rendezvous spot for a final destination further into major cities of the Northeast. Most of the team agreed that if the men had remained in Clemson during the past two weeks, it would explain why the checkpoints on the interstates had not produced results. Either these people were extremely clever or his guys were inept. After three weeks, due to the lack of activity and the two agency's workload in other places, it was decided to reduce the taskforce in Clemson to one agent. This agent's job would be to scrutinize the photos of new driver's license applications and monitor new hires of local contractors.

CHAPTER 45

Football in America

As June turned into July in 2008, the construction delays at the stadium became more urgent. Football season was only eight weeks away. All constraints on the number of construction workers had been removed. Therefore it had not been difficult for Lotcho to secure jobs for all eleven of his team at the stadium construction site. His decision to remain flexible had paid off. It was a perfect set-up for his team to become familiar with the stadium's infrastructure. The plan was proceeding even better than he had dared hope. Because keys to the doors were an important part of the plan, when a set of master keys were left laying on a desk long enough for one of the team members to make a wax imprint, he could not believe their good fortune. Allah was definitely with the S-Team. That evening, back at the house they all had a good laugh, over dinner, about how stupid the infidels were. Each week when the team was paid, Lotcho would collect the cash and head straight to the 'job finder' to pay him what was owed for his finder's fee. Lotcho never let the 'job finder' actually see him. He would put the cash in an envelope and place it in a prearranged location.

The team was living in two houses, situated near each other. They had strict instructions from Lotcho never to be seen in a large group. They went back and forth between houses after dark and never went to work or came home the same way. They had learned that there was a woman with an old van that went around town and picked up Mexicans and dropped them off at their job sites. She would stop at different grocery stores for them to pick up food. This soon became their transportation of choice. The men were careful to be picked up and dropped off at different locations. The woman did not ask questions and did not attempt conversation with her passengers. The FBI agents in Clemson never became aware of this transportation process. As the one remaining agent monitored the DMV and contractor records, he was oblivious to the S-Team and their activities. Unknowingly, the contractors aided the S-Team in their mission. Because contractors needed illegal workers to complete their projects on time and on budget, they made sure the agent did not see any records that might look suspicious.

This August turned out to be one of the hottest months on record in Clemson. It was good thing for the 'S' team, because heat did not bother them. None of the 11 men complained about long days, and because of this, they were given additional hours. They were hard workers and did not draw the attention of others. The first football game was held on August 30th despite the delayed construction. That Saturday, the 'S' team were not scheduled to work, so they all went to the game, leaving the house in pairs and buying their tickets from scalpers just outside the gates. Because these men were not familiar with American football, the experience astonished them. It seemed every single person entering the stadium was wearing the same bright colored shirts and hats. The noise level in the stadium was louder than anything they had ever experienced.

The opposing team ran out on to the field from underneath the West end stand to a few boos from the audience. The 'S'-Team was accosted by the unfamiliar aroma of popcorn, French fries and pizza. What a unique experience this was turning out to be.

Suddenly, the University's band blared the team's theme song. That loud music in concert with the sudden noise of the crowd, who was instantly on their feet yelling wildly at the top of their lungs, startled the men. Just as the S-Team was becoming accustomed to one new experience, yet another confronted their senses. Although they had been well trained to blend into the crowd, the sudden explosion of a cannon, the smoke blowing across the field and thousands of roaring fans had them shaking in fear. They did not know what to make of all this noise and confusion. For a few moments, the S-Team thought the stadium had been attacked by someone else. Then to top off this experience, thousands of brightly colored balloons, were released into the blue summer sky and at that moment, the local football team appeared at the top of the hill, ran under the big score board and down the grassy bank onto the ball field. The band jumped up and down to the sound of the deep base tuba turning right, and then left, as the band continued to pump out the theme song and the seventy-eight thousand fans were screaming to the tops of their voices. 'S team' took all of this in and slowly realized that in a few short months, they would be the unwanted center of all this attention. Slowly, each of the men realized that their mission had probability for a successful outcome.

  At half time, as planned, the 'S' Team fanned out and went to their pre-assigned gates. They were observing the traffic flow and the security at each gate. They observed everyone in uniform to see if they carried a weapon. Security that afternoon was a mixture of sheriff's deputies and highway patrolmen mingling with the crowd. The team was surprised by their casual attitude. Most were just standing talking with each other and earning extra off-duty cash. Even more surprising was the gate security. These were mostly old men with un-official uniforms and no weapons. Each team member carefully observed the best place to stand to remain out of the cross hairs of a marksman. There were a lot of large concrete columns and walls one could stand behind. As they considered the day they would execute their mission, they saw how

Soft Target
by Larry Greer

they could turn the panicked crowd back into the stadium with just a few burst of fire into the air.

No one took notice of the twelve men casing the crowd. One key element to the plan was the dramatic entrance of the players running down the hill before the game. This would make the unexpected entrance of the buses with the players still on board even more exciting to the fans. They speculated that few spectators would notice the men standing in the shadows dressed in all black head to toe. Even the security would be trying to get a view of the players arriving onto the field in a very different way. This would put many of the security men on the inside of the stadium entrances and at a definite disadvantage.

After the game, the 'S'team broke up into small groups. They decided to get something to eat before returning home. There were thousands of people gathering around the big stadium, eating, drinking and rehashing the game. With so many people focused on this sporting event, no one took notice of them.

Being the first game of the season, John and Molly Massey had driven down from Virginia to see their son Jason play in his first game of the season. As expected, Hartwell came out on top and the extra points kicked by Jason had made the deciding difference. John and Molly were both proud and excited. Before leaving Washington, they reminded family and friends to be sure they watched the game on ESPN and to look for Jason.

In the back of John's mind, he was remembering that Clemson had been the point of interest for their recent FBI and CIA investigation. He could not help but look around and scan the faces in the crowd. He was not sure he could pick an Arab out of this large crowd. Surprisingly, there were a large number of ethnic faces among the fans.

Soft Target
by Larry Greer

Jason was anxious to meet his folks later that night, but being a typical college student, he first wanted to join his teammates at the local pub. Meeting at this pub was an old school tradition. It was the team's time to celebrate their win and rehash the game.

Several hours later, Jason joined his parents at the pizza parlor, bringing with him a teammate who had become a good friend in the first few weeks of school. It was an animated conversation, discussing each and every play of the game... what had been executed well or screwed up. For John and Molly, this was a continuation of the discussions they had enjoyed after Jason's high school football games.

In spite of this comradery, John could not totally focus on the conversation. His focus was on the Arabs that Homeland Security had been looking for in this very small town. Every time a dark-skinned person crossed past their table, he tried to lock their face into his memory. Were they Arab? Mexican? Indian? Suddenly, he realized that he was staring into the half closed eyes of a young man sitting two tables over. Their eyes locked for a moment before the other man turned away. He was in the company of two other men of similar in age and appearance.

John, himself, looked down at his plate. He was embarrassed, and at the same time had a strange sensation that this was significant. Almost as if beyond their power to turn away, they both had intently stared into the other's eyes, trying to figure out thoughts and purpose in this small town. John chided himself: *I must be working too hard. I am beginning to see buggers behind bushes.*

What were the odds that Lotcho/Mohamed of Pakistan and John Massey, of the FBI would come face to face?

Soft Target
by Larry Greer

CHAPTER 46

Preparation

Three months later, on a warm November day, the Friday front page headline read: **State Comes to Hartwell as Underdog**. The twelve members of the 'S' team were all together this morning in one of the two houses they occupied. The newspaper was passed around the kitchen table. Team members were in a subdued mood and did not have a lot to say as they sipped their morning tea. They would not report for work today as Lotcho wanted for the last time, to rehearse tomorrow's plan. What had never been discussed was their exit plan. Each and every man knew that in all likelihood tomorrow would be the end for them and they would die martyrs. Even if their plan was successful, there would be no way out. No way out of the stadium, out of South Carolina or out of America. When the time came, they would kill as many of the infidels as possible before being killed themselves.

During the previous week, Lotcho had given Raga and Johey the address of a garage that was way out in the country and surrounded by junk cars and trucks. They were told that they would find a red, white and blue cement truck among the wrecked cars and trucks in this junkyard. Lotcho instructed them to borrow a small pickup from one of their Mexican co-workers. Pay him for use of the truck for a few hours on Saturday morning and pick up the guns and explosives hidden inside the belly of the cement mixer.

Soft Target
by Larry Greer

Jack Harper had pulled the cement truck behind his Peterbilt wrecker down I-95 without incident. He had been told by Harry to deliver the cement truck and an envelope containing two hundred dollars, to the garage owner. Payment was to store the cement truck for a month. Jack told the garage owner that someone would come by and check on the truck within the next couple of weeks.

Raga and Johey had found the garage and colorfully-painted cement truck without any trouble. The garage was closed and the owner nowhere around. They opened the make-shift hatch on the bottom side of the mixer barrel and with the aid of a flashlight they could see the boxes of dynamite and black trash bags they knew held the machine pistols and ammunition. The boxes and bags had been secured to the bottom of the barrel. After checking to make sure there was no one around and quickly loaded their cargo into the pickup.

When they arrived at the house, everything was quickly unloaded in the garage at the back of the house. Three of the men unpacked the guns and checked out the explosives. In one box Lotcho found the remote control which was a cell phone and responder that he would use to active the dynamite if it became necessary. He took the batteries out of the cell phone and receiver. He replaced them with fresh batteries. This thorough attention to detail was one of the things that had made Lotcho such a natural to lead the mission. The men had purchased four large ice chests and a charcoal grill. The ice chests were used to repack the dynamite along with explosive caps including a remote control receiver. The lids were secured with a plastic straps. Once the plastic cords were wrapped around the ice chests, no one could open the chests without cutting the straps. This ensured that the precious cargo would be safe from unwanted intruders. The grill and charcoal were for appearances only. Anyone at the stadium would see them as just another group of tailgaters. Typical tailgating food, like potato chips, would be tucked around the chests to make it look legitimate. Lotcho checked out each pistol before passing them out to his men.

As crowded as the first game in August had been, the S-Team had learned over the past two months that tickets to this cross-state rivalry game were almost impossible to get. Valdess had told Lotcho that he needed to be prepared to pay a high price for them. As it turned out, the 'job finder' had a few connections and for one hundred dollars each, could get them twelve tickets. Everything seemed to be falling into place for Lotcho and his team.

Once the weapons had been distributed, Lotcho asked them to gather in the living room. They were to rehearse the plans for one last time. Lotcho began,

"It is now 9:00am which makes it 33 hours until kick off time. Tomorrow afternoon at 3:00pm everyone except Raga and Johey will ride with the lady who has the van that took us to work every day. She will drop us off at the stadium while you, Raga and Johey, will take the fully loaded truck to the West end parking lot area. Johey, before you enter the stadium, you will get out of the truck and walk. You will walk through the parking lot, find a car that is not locked and steal a parking pass near the spot where we need you to park the truck. Then Johey, you will take the parking pass to Raga, who will be waiting just outside the stadium lot. Make sure your stolen parking pass is prominently displayed on the driver's side of the windshield. Smile confidently at the guard and proceed to the West End lot, parking in the designated construction spot.

The rest of us will ride as far as we can and at 5:00pm, seven men, one at a time, will go to the ground level entrance that construction workers have been using below the West end stands.

Use the copied door key and enter the construction area. Because it is the last big game, there will not be any workers in this area. You will head directly to the small storage room as we rehearsed. The same key will open this door. Two days ago, we placed twelve large pizza boxes in that storage room. Use these boxes to hide your pistols. Double check to make sure that your ticket is in your pocket. The stub must already be torn off. That way if you are asked to show your ticket, it looks like you have been in the stadium and are just going back in. After having set up your chairs you will wait until precisely 5:10pm. Then each of you grab a trash bag containing our guns and bring them in and come to the storage room where the rest of us will be waiting. Make very sure no one is paying attention to what you are doing. Johey, make sure you do not forget to put the note that I gave you on the windshield. This note will tell people your 'construction truck' is broken and you will be back in ten minutes.

"At 5:45, the Hartwell football team will start coming out of the players exit from under the West End Stands and begin to board the buses. Three of us will stand by the storage room door and watch for our time to be the last ones to run out and board each bus. Raga you Joey will head for the communication rooms. You both have a key to get in these rooms. Remember, once you are in these rooms; make sure to lock the door behind you. At that point you will brandish your gun and if there is anyone in the room besides the technician and cameraman, order them to sit in the corner on the floor and be still or you will shoot them. These same instructions are for both the communications room and the media room next door." Lotcho pointed to one of the other men. "Jarray, you will post yourself outside the two rooms to keep people from attempting to enter. The remaining eight of you will go to your assigned gate and watch for the three buses to appear on the playing field. That will take place at approximately 5:55pm. At that time, remove your outer layer of clothes and expose your black outfit as well as your guns. Force anyone around the stadium

Soft Target
by Larry Greer

gates to go back into the stands. When all three of the buses are on the field, Johey, you will make sure the technician has the camera on the first bus. I want the camera to be able to see me thru the front windshield. Raga, you make sure that the Homeland Security hot line is live so that what I have to say will be heard by the government as well as everyone in the stadium. This is extremely critical. I will have my wireless microphone in my pocket as well as the remote for the dynamite. Make sure you have the DVD that I may have to ask you to play. Instruct the technician to set up a split screen in order for the network to show a live broadcast. My intention is to get the President of the United States on that screen and into a dialog with me. We have all practiced dry runs of this plan many times. We have studied it on paper and we have made ourselves very familiar with the stadium over the past three months. We are being charged by our leader with a very important mission. The time is now to honor Allah. If any of you have questions, speak now!" Silence filled the room.
"OK since you are all comfortable with your roles, let's break up into groups of four. We will mingle with the crowd in town and watch the parade and fire works. You have worked hard and so far, our plan has been executed smoothly. You deserve a reward, so go in your groups of four for pizza and a beer?"

CHAPTER 47

John & Molly

John and Molly Massey had waited all season for this epic match between the two rival schools. Jason had performed well as the team's first string kicker and John could not be prouder of his son. Because this was such an important game for Jason, John had Jason purchase tickets his brother and sister-in-law, so they could see their nephew in action. They all arrived in Clemson Friday afternoon so that they might visit with Jason for a short time that day. The coach had them on a rigid schedule the day before this big game. The team was not allowed off campus after the dinner hour. This had been a perfect season and the coach was not going to allow pre-game revelry to spoil the most unpredictable game of the year. Jason had been able to get the four tickets on the thirty yard line about ten rows up on the Hartwell side.

Jason's family joined him in the school dining room. For the final match of the season, this was tradition for the players and their families. All conversation centered on the next day's game and predictions of victory. Jason modestly told his family that game films they had watch made him feel it would be close. Nervously, he voiced a hope that he could have at least 75% kicking accuracy. With all of Jason's success, John was proud of his son for not letting that go to his head.

Soft Target
by Larry Greer

After a jovial dinner, they left campus, checked into their hotel and decided to meet up for a few drinks. Even with all the family excitement and anticipation about tomorrow, John could never really relax and leave his job behind. Molly frequently chided him about constantly checking his BlackBerry. Even tonight he was guilty of this.

As they sat at a noisy lounge on Main Street in Clemson, John, out of habit, checked for messages. He notice one from Milton and immediately opened the email. Milton was encouraging him to enjoy the game, but keep an eye out for 'S1'. Although he added that he was only joking, John had to admit that he was already doing just that.

CHAPTER 48

Game Day

At six a.m. Saturday morning, the 'S' team was up and ready to go. As had been their habit for all of their lives, they kneeled on their prayer rugs, facing Mecca and prayed. Many of them thought that this might be their last prayer to Allah and each in his own way prayed for today's success. As they prayed they thought of their families who most had not seen in over two years. As each man rose from his rug, he repeated the familiar: "Praise be to Allah and Allah is great".

After prayers and a final check to make sure they had everything they needed for their mission, they walked to the larger house, which had come to be known as the main house. Although each of the two houses held six men, the "main house" was larger and had been their gathering place. As they had done for the past four months, they selected a spot on the floor of the main room. They formed a circle and passed around the pot of tea. The conversation was subdued. With the mission only hours away each man was dealing with his own thoughts. They knew their jobs well and did not need to go through the plan again. Today Lotcho required that they fast. He knew there would be many nervous stomachs and that included his.

At two o'clock that afternoon, they made final preparations to leave the house for the last time. Even though this was an evening game, fans were beginning to gather on the streets walking toward the stadium. At the last minute, Lotcho had decided they would not ride with the lady in the van today, but join the crowd in the streets, walking toward the stadium. Only Johey and Raga would be riding. They slid into the seats of the rented truck and headed to their parking place near the stadium to wait. Before stepping out of the house at exactly 3:00pm, Lotcho asked that they form a circle.

"Today, my brothers, we will make our people proud. We will be seen live on big screens around the world as no others has ever been. We will prove to the world that al-Qaeda was not defeated in Iraq. Our movement is strong and will live on till we have conquered the infidels around the world. One great man had this dream and we are but instruments to carry out his plan. Praise Allah for he is great."

Soft Target
by Larry Greer

CHAPTER 49

Mr. President

President of the United States, Evan White had arrived in Texas early Saturday morning. He had always loved his ranch and relished the days he could change into outdoor work clothes and forget that he was Commander in Chief. He had known this job was the most stressful job in the world, but the reality of that constant stress had taken a toll on him and his family. He found getting the chain saw out and cutting underbrush and improving the trails around the ranch, allowed his body and his head to forget Washington. He wanted to get in a little work down around the pond before his weekend guests showed up later that afternoon. Their plan was for a relaxed weekend watching football and grilling steaks. He was proud of the new high tech stainless steel grill and looked forward to firing it up. He told the cook to take the night off. The normalcy involved with preparing a simple meal of steak and potatoes, was exactly what he needed. The First Lady's job was to make the salad.

The Secretary of Defense and her husband would arrive around two o'clock and they would start the evening with drinks and appetizers on the veranda. His plan was to have dinner around seven. It was the middle of his second term. This was the time the political machine considered him a "lame duck." He spent more time than he liked doing political fundraisers. He worked hard to remain above the political fray so that he would leave the party with sufficient funding and high ratings for the next man to follow.

Soft Target
by Larry Greer

Shortly after the beginning of his first term, the *nine eleven* attack turned everything upside down. Not since the Pearl Harbor attack, had the United States been attacked by a foreign nation on our soil. The outrage from American citizens had been just as ferocious after *Nine-Eleven* as it had been after the Japanese attacked Pearl Harbor. Being a historian, he often thought about what it must have been like for FDR and also for Lincoln. He likened these times in history to the present. The difference today, was that anyone could say whatever he felt without repercussions. President White had aged over the past seven and a half years, but that always came with the territory. He had started out with a full head of black hair. Now his hair was gray and thinning.

Around one thirty, a secret service agent let President White know that the Defense Secretary and her husband were at the airport and would be arriving soon. This meant that his few enjoyable hours of ranch work were over. He put the chain saw into the truck and headed for the house. How he missed driving his beloved truck.

The Secretary of Defense, Sally Robb and her husband, Philip arrived before The President had a chance to shower and change. As she always did, his beloved wife was a perfect hostess. Drinks were offered and everyone settled into the spacious media room in preparation for the game. Although Even White did not drink, he made sure his bar was well stocked and no matter what type of drink his guests wanted, it was available. He walked into the room and both Sally and Philip stood to greet the President. Evan was still enjoying the casual afternoon and so responded to their greeting with his standard Texas "Howdy."

The President's media room was set up with four enormous flat screen televisions. He loved college football and could watch multiple games at the same time. This set up was also convenient for conference meetings with participants in many parts of the world.

Although a full detail of secret service agents were on duty, their presence was never obvious. The secret service command center was conveniently located in the room next to the media center. That command center housed the fabled 'Red phone'. This secure line allowed the President to talk directly with NORAD, the Central Defense Command Center at the core of Cheyenne Mountain in Colorado and every member of his cabinet. In times of emergency, the media room at the ranch instantly became 'command central' for the President. After *Nine-Eleven,* President White had insisted that every member of his cabinet be available at a moment's notice.

At 4:30pm central time, the President invited Sally and Philip to join him for some of the pregame shows. Sally and Philip were guests of President White that weekend because they all enjoyed college football and the two had become good friends of he and the First Lady. It was 5:30pm eastern time and the Hartwell vs. State game kicked off at six o'clock. The President told Sally and Philip that one of his top CIA men, John Massey had a son who had demonstrated exceptional skills this year as a kicker. He shared that Massey was the Call Center Director and was a valuable asset to the Agency.

It was now thirty minutes before game time in Clemson, South Carolina.

CHAPTER 50

In Position

The 'S' team had woven in among the fans walking toward the stadium. Although this walk was less than a mile, it would take almost one hour. They walked in groups of two or three and said very little to each other. They were all preoccupied with their own thoughts. From the age of ten, they had studied the Koran. Their training had taught them that the way to heaven was to serve Allah. In their minds, they were sure these were their last glorious hours on this earth. As faithful Muslims, they felt honored to have been selected for this mission, but as mortal men, they still felt trepidation at the thought of their actions over the coming hours.

At five minutes after four, they arrived at the stadium grounds. As they walked toward the West End stadium parking area, several passed close by an ice cream vendor. It would have been a temptation to have one final cone of ice cream, a treat they had come to enjoy during their time in America. However, they reluctantly passed him by and headed directly up the hill to sit in the shade of a few trees. As instructed, at exactly five o'clock they started back down the hill towards the employee entrance on the West End. As they walked near the West End parking lot, they could see that the construction parking space was still open. It took them less than ten minutes to walk down the short embankment and enter the employee door. Not one of the hundreds of tailgaters milling about took any notice.

Soft Target
by Larry Greer

At exactly 5:10p,, Raga and Johey drove to West End parking entrance where a highway patrolman held up his hand to indicate they should stop. Raga smiled and pointed at the parking pass that was hanging on the rear view mirror. The patrolman took a second look and momentarily looked puzzled. However, because of the crowds, he waved them on and Raga and Johey breathed a sigh of relief. Raga smiled again and thanked the patrolman. Johey had successfully lifted the parking pass off a car where about fifty people were concentrating on the activities of tailgating in the humid 90^0 weather. They were drinking, cooking on their grills and sharing sports stories. No one had given him a second look as he reached into the car and slipped the parking pass into his pocket.

By 5:18pm the other nine members of the S-Team had successfully slipped into the lower level maintenance room of the West End stadium. When the door knob turned, everyone froze. As Raga and Johey slipped in with their two black garbage bags, the other nine members gave a sigh of relief. The black bags held the machine pistols critical to their mission. Each pistol had been fully loaded the night before. There were also two extra clips for each gun. The room was dim and the 12 men were almost shoulder to shoulder in the small room. They pulled the pizza boxes off the shelf. Each man released the safeties of his gun and placed his pistol in a pizza box.

"Did you leave the note on the truck as I ask you to?" Lotcho inquired.
"Yes, and we did not see anyone around the truck that might question the note," responded Johey.

Soft Target
by Larry Greer

CHAPTER 51

Pre-Game

At 5:30pm the pre-game show kicked off festivities with the college band marching up and down the field. The crowd was getting all wound up for a game they had anticipated for an entire football season and even beyond. For decades this rivalry was the culmination of college football competition in South Carolina. No one could ever predict who would win this game regardless of either team's record. The stadium was known as one of the loudest in the county. It was was frequently full for any game, but this particular game maxed out capacity every year it was played in Clemson. If you didn't have season tickets, you watched it on television. Almost everyone in the State was focused on this competition.

John and Molly Massey, along with John's brother and sister-in-law had taken their seats. John was wearing a jacket to conceal his Glock. Even this late in the season, his heavy jacket was more than he needed in the warm November afternoon. His job required him to declare his weapon. Once he let authorities at the gate know, it had taken over ten minutes to get through security, even at the VIP gate. John was tense, waiting for Jason to run down that hill in a cloud of glory. If Hartwell lost the toss, Jason would be the one to make the first kick to State. While John was sitting there, he fired off a text to Milt.

"Watch the game, it will be a good one and be sure to cheer for Jason."

Soft Target
by Larry Greer

There was a ten hour difference between Pakistan and South Carolina. On the opposite side of the world, two men were also anxiously waiting for the game to start. It was 7:00am, their time. It is not known whether the Commander had access to a television, but Valdess was sitting by his TV alone in his office at the Camp. He had not been in communication with Mohamed since leaving Clemson three months before and despite all their preparation, he was nervous, as the clock counted down to 8:00am. It would be the culmination of many years of intensive planning, training and programming.

The President, the First Lady and their guests sat in the big Lazy Boy chairs in the media room. The President and Philip were talking football and he tried repeatedly to get some kind of a bet going. But, Philip was holding out for more points.
"Come on Phil, you know he's not going to make it easy for you to win. Be a sport. You are making a hundred dollars sound like a thousand, cajoled Sally."

Back in South Carolina, Larry Howard, the stadium manager, had just received a concerning report from one of his employees. Evidently several people had been seen going in the employee door on the ground level of the new West End section and there was an unauthorized pickup truck parked in the construction zone. Larry emphasized with the employee that a key was needed to get in that door. If someone did not have a key, then it must have been left open.
"Maybe some kid jammed the lock so he could let his buddies sneak in" the employee offered.

Larry responded that he was in the middle of something important and would get down there as soon as possible, but probably not before the pre-game activities were over.

CHAPTER 52

The Mission In Action

I no longer needed my alias and could again assume my given name, Mohamed. I was very relieved for that small change. I noticed it was 5:45pm on the nose. I turned to Razza and ask if he and Imran were ready. The team all put their hands on the other's shoulders and repeated, "Praise to Allah." It was a solemn moment and the last we knew we would have together.

Razza and Imran nodded to let me know they were ready.

I cracked open the storage room door where we were huddled in the bowels of the new West End stands. Hoping that no one would be in the hall, I peeked out. Allah was with us. The coast was clear, so the three of us slipped out to the side door that allowed us a view of the area where the players would board their buses. The players were milling around, nervously waiting for their moment to shine. A loud voice could be heard above their conversation and called for them to "load up". The plan called for me to board the first bus with Razza on the second and Imran on the third. The engines were running to maintain the air-conditioning. Despite the November date, it had been a hot afternoon.

Just as the last players were getting on board, I gave the order to board.
"LET'S GO"

Soft Target
by Larry Greer

The three of us ran the short two hundred feet to the buses. Just as the last player got on, I gave his back a hard push, propelling him into the bus and yelled out.

"SIT DOWN AND DO AS I SAY AND NO ONE WILL GET HURT!! As for you (and I pointed his gun in the driver's face,) YOU do as you are told or you will be shot!"

The player's faces displayed first a look of confusion. That quickly changed to expressions of shock and then horror. They could not believe what was happening. I could hear a mummer among several in the back of the bus. I had anticipated this and in a loud voice I directed my comments to the linebackers seated at the back of the bus.
"KEEP YOUR MOUTHS SHUT! DO NOT LOOK AT ANYONE EXCEPT ME OR YOU DIE. --- DRIVER, MOVE OUT AS YOU ALWAYS DO AND STOP AT EAST END SCOREBOARD."

I had changed to the all-black clothing, as planned. I both felt and looked like the terrorists that had been depicted on television in America since *Nine-Eleven*. The players were terrified, remembering what had happened at another college a couple of years ago when over thirty students had been murdered by a lone gunman. The driver was an elderly man whose hands were shaking so hard, he had to take a firm grip on the steering wheel to calm himself. As instructed by me, he drove slowly out of the parking lot and onto the street. The highway patrolmen did not see the look of panic on the bus drivers faces as they drove by. He also did not take notice of the man in black brandishing a pistol. The players began to realize the severity of this situation and Mohamed noticed that some of their faces had transformed from looks of horror to expressions of hatred. Jason Massey, the young kicker, was on the front seat closest to me. I recognized him as the red-shirted sophomore who had been credited with kicking the winning score at several games this year. I was leaning against the dash of the bus safely out of reach of any player that thought he could be a hero. I recognized this look in Jason's eyes. I warned Jason,

"DON'T TRY IT. I WILL NOT HESITATE FOR A SECOND TO BLOW YOUR HEAD OFF! AND THAT GOES FOR ANY ONE OF YOU THAT HAS SOMETHING HEROIC ON YOUR MIND."

The buses belching out their diesel smoke crept slowly out into the street, one closely behind the other and headed up the hill along the north side of the stadium, passing hundreds of fans that had a habit of waiting outside to cheer on their team. Something was different today. The players who normally waved back were looking straight ahead and did not seem to notice the fans. This puzzled some fans, but in the frenzy of the event, none of them noticed the man in black at the front of the bus. The first bus made its last right turn and slowly approached its normal parking spot that had been blocked off for the three buses. As we stopped, hundreds of fans began to close in, waiting for the whistle that signaled the players to emerge from the bus and charge down the hill. This was the beginning of a very crazy, chaotic afternoon for fans and players alike. These ardent fans knew the routine, but something was amiss. The first bus had deviated from its routine stop.

Mohamed instructed the driver in a clear but intimidating voice,

"I WANT YOU TO TAKE A WIDE TURN, AND DRIVE CARFULLY UNDER THE SCORE BOARD AND DOWN THE BANK AND ONTO THE MIDDLE OF THE FIELD. IS THERE ANYTHING YOU DO NOT UNDERSTAND ABOUT MY ORDER?"

Soft Target
by Larry Greer

The driver responded in a weak, stuttering voice, looking only out of the corner of his eye at me.

"But-but-I have never done this before. I do not even know if the bus will go under the scoreboard?" As he spoke, I could see tears forming in the old man's eyes.
"YOU HEARD ME OLD MAN. DO WHAT I SAID…NOW! TAKE A WIDE TURN AND HEAD DOWN THE BANK. YOU WILL NEED TO BLOW YOUR HORN IF YOU DON'T WANT TO RUN OVER THE IDIOTS STANDING IN THE WAY."

The driver took a deep breath. He snuck a quick look in the rear view mirror. He had been responsible for driving the short trip around the stadium for many years and had developed affection for these players. In his mind, they were HIS boys. As he made the wide turn, the bus hit the curb straight on. It bounced up over the curb and as it passed under the scoreboard, it narrowly missed grazing the bottom of the board. Once under the scoreboard, the steep bank and the playing field came into immediate view. Over eighty thousand fans were there standing and awaiting the arrival of their team. By contrast, the players were feeling nauseated and traumatized. Jason actually had the crazy thought that this could be a big prank being pulled by STATE, but he had quickly put that notion out of his mind as the bus began the slow downward roll towards the middle of the field. The driver laid on the horn and fans scatted in every direction. There was a panicked yell from the players as the bus slid down the grassy slope at a severe angle. This was the first noise from the players since Mohamed had entered the bus. The driver applied his breaks, but too late. The goal post was directly ahead. The bus slammed into the goal posts and they collapsed in pieces around the bus. Not understanding the situation, but realizing it was time for players to be on the field, those holding onto the helium balloons had released them and the cannon fired at the same instant. Now the band added to the

Soft Target
by Larry Greer

pandemonium with a loud rendition of the fight song. But as the crowd realized something was different, and maybe not right, they quickly quieted, waiting to see what was going to happen. Suddenly, you could only hear whispers, as the crowd tried to understand why the buses were on the field. The crowd stood in shock and surprise as the first bus crashed thru the goal post and drove to the center of the field, finally stopping at an angle facing the South Stands. The other two buses navigated around the demolished goal posts and followed suit down the field, turning in the same direction they came to a stop beside each other.

Bill Morrow's family had owned season tickets to these games for several generations. They never missed a home game. Bill leaned toward his wife Carol and whispered,

"What in the Hell is going on. This can't have been planned! They just ran over the Damn goal post!!"

There were similar questions coming from all over the big stadium. And suddenly the quiet crowd erupted into angry shouts. Bill noticed one of his friends running along the Hartwell sideline with his fists in the air and yelling at the first bus,
"What in the shit do you think you are doing?"

Bill pointed out his friend to Carol and shook his head. "Boy I'll bet Silky is going to let somebody have it when this is over."

Simultaneously to this pandemonium, Raga burst into the communications room located above the south side stands, he was glad to find only three people in the room. He pointed to the third man,

"MOVE TO THE LEFT SIDE OF THE ROOM AND SIT ON THE FLOOR. IF YOU MOVE FROM THAT SPOT, I WILL

Soft Target
by Larry Greer

KILL YOU, UNDERSTAND? NOW, YOU AT THE CONTROL BOARDS, ARE TO DO EXACTLY AS I TELL YOU. IS THAT CLEAR?"

All three men were in astonishment. The technician did as he was told, fearing for his life. While Raga instructed the technician to put the camera on the first bus and project it onto the score board. Johey told his technician in the other media room, to turn on the remote mike designated for the head referee to communicate to the crowd.

"I WANT IT TO BE TURNED UP SO IT CAN BE HEARD THROUGHOUT THE STADIUM!" Johey directed.

Raga told the cameraman to zoom in tight on the first bus, so that the man in black could be seen clearly. Now on the big screen for the first time, the crowd could see a man wearing a mask and dressed totally in black and holding up what appeared to be a gun. When this happened, those who had considered this a hoax of some kind quickly dismissed the thought. Again the crowd noise quieted, as they realized something really bad was developing! Almost simultaneously, everyone in the crowd knew they needed to get out of the stadium. People ran toward the tunnel exits, fighting to get past each other. In the mayhem, many were knocked out of the way and down the steps. Those first into tunnel exits thought they could run straight to their cars. This is where they ran directly into more men dressed in black. These men had machine pistols aimed at their heads. This sight caused further panic and now they didn't know which way to go. However, it quickly became clear that they were to head back into the stadium seats or it they would be shot where they stood. Those still outside the stadium had already taken off for their cars. Although they couldn't see what was going on inside, they knew the noise and confusion could not be good. The sheriff's deputies and highway patrolmen were also in a state of confusion. At first the panicking fans told them that there was a gunman at the main entrance to the

Soft Target
by Larry Greer

North Stands and so they began to run in that direction and then another report said that there was a gunman at one of the South Stadium entrances. It quickly developed into total chaos among the various law enforcement agencies. The patrolmen on the inside the stadium could not get close to the exits because panicked fans had them blocked. If they moved into those crowds, they would be in danger of being trampled to death themselves. They could not get a clear shot of the gunmen at the tunnel entrances. They were trapped just as everyone else inside.

John Massey was totally confused by what was developing. He knew that his son Jason was in the first bus, but there was no way he could get to him. Besides he could see the man in black on the screen standing in the first bus. He put his hand on Molly's head and pushed her down on the floor and directed her to stay down. He grabbed his BlackBerry and fired off a message to Milt who was at his home in Maryland.

"Title: URGENT! Milton, it appears that terrorists are in this football stadium with guns and as crazy as it might seem, they are holding the players hostage in the middle of the field on the buses. HLC and state officials should be contacted immediately."

Milton had been watching the pregame activities when suddenly the screen had gone blank with a message that the network was experiencing temporary difficulties.
Milton felt his BlackBerry vibrate in his pocket. As was his habit, he read most messages immediately. This one he had to read twice. This explains why the network had gone blank. He immediately, forwarded John's e-mail to Joe Black with the FBI.

Joe was shocked by John's email, but not totally surprised. He immediately notified Homeland Security and South Carolina FBI. At this point no one knew the full picture. What did these men want? Black decided it would be prudent to contact Bill

Houser who was Chief of Staff at the White House. He was certain the President would want to know what was happening. Then he e-mailed John Massey and asked to be kept in the loop. John called Black immediately.

"Director Black, this is John Massey."
"John, what the Hell is happening?"
"It appears we are all being held hostage. It looks like we have more than one gunman in the stadium."
"What makes you think that?"

"From what I can observe, people have jammed the exits and seem to be at a stand still. They are not moving at all out of any exit; in fact many are heading back into the stadium. It is pure pandemonium in here, Director."

"John, anything else seem to be unusual? Are there demands being made by the gunmen?"

"All I can tell you is that the score board appears to be blinking, as if someone is trying to change the settings. There is also a static on the sound system. Hold on Director, there is now a picture on the screen. There is a close up of one of the buses and I can now see a man in a black mask with a gun. It looks like he is attempting to make a broadcast to the entire stadium. If you have a TV close by turn it on to ESPN and see if they are broadcasting what I am looking at."

"Hold on a minute." Black ran and grabbed the remote. He put the channel on ESPN as John recommended.

"Oh, my God! I can see the score board and the bus. John, this is serious."

Soft Target
by Larry Greer

CHAPTER 53

Al Qaeda Strikes Again

The minute Bill Houser, Chief of Staff, saw the incoming call from Joe Black he headed directly to the Control Center in the White House basement. He barked to the technicians,

"Bring up the ESPN, right now!" Something big is going wrong in Clemson, South Carolina."

It only took a few moments to determine that this was an event he needed to make the President aware of. At the Texas ranch, the phone rang only twice on the Presidents special phone.

"Yes"
"Mr. President, this is Houser"
President Evan White knew that Bill did not call him on weekends without good reason.
"Are you watching the Hartwell game sir?"

"We just sat down and I turned several games on. Hartwell was not coming through on the ESPN, so I changed the channel. What's wrong?"

"Sir, you need to turn it back right now. There is a major emergency going on in that stadium. Gunmen are holding the players hostage in their team buses. And the spectators are captive inside the stadium as well."

"My God, Bill. Has anyone been hurt?"
"No sir, not yet."

The President had turned his channel back to ESPN, that had the Hartwell game scheduled and he could now see all that Bill Houser was talking about.

"Mr. President, I am confident that Homeland Security is already on top of this, but no one knows what these gunmen want. I recommend, Mr. President, that you and the Secretary of Defense get into the situation room and we will get the CIA and FBI on a conference phone with Homeland Security."

"Yes, Bill, make it happen. Sally and I will be waiting." Sally was already absorbing the events at the Hartwell Stadium and did not need to be brought up to speed.

Soft Target
by Larry Greer

CHAPTER 54

The Demands

There was now a groundswell of human anxiety that demonstrated itself in crowd noise like a freight train deep in the night rising in volume as the confusion grew. Then the stadium speakers screeched as they do when volume adjustments are being made.

The voices of the 84,000 fans instantly quelled, as they waited to see what would happen next. Who would be speaking and what would happen?

Mohamed fumbled with the remote microphone and as he took it out of his pocket he thought,

"I hope Raga has done his job correctly and this thing works." He tapped the mike and heard the thump of the mike respond from all speakers. He put it to his lips to test it again with a puff of air. Again he thought, "I'm not sure if I needed that second test or if I'm stalling. It is now or never!" Before he spoke, he looked directly into Jason's eyes. His look of revulsion gave Mohamed resolve. He wanted to communicate to Jason with his expression: 'I am keeping an eye on you and if you so as make a move, you will be the first to die." Then Mohamed looked up to his left and could see his image larger than life on the screen. This was the moment that his team had prepared for. Mohamed had never made a speech to more than his eleven team members, but here he was before 84,000 captive listeners and hopefully millions of viewers around the world.

As Mohamed began to speak, the President of the United States was at his ranch in Texas glued to the screen in the situation room. Mohamed's words resounded throughout the stadium,

"I COME HERE AS A REPRESENTIVE OF THE COMMANDER OF AL-QAEDA. I HAVE MANY OF MY BROTHERS WITH ME HERE TONIGHT IN THIS STADIUM. WE COME AS MESSENGERS OF ALLAH. KNOW NOW THAT YOU HAVE NOT DEFEATED US IN IRAQ OR ANYWHERE ELSE IN THE WORLD. AS YOU CAN SEE FOR YOURSELVES, WE WALK AMONG YOU. THE PERSON THAT IS STANDING NEXT TO YOU COULD VERY WELL BE A MEMBER OF ONE OF OUR MANY BRETHREN. THEY ONLY AWAIT ORDERS FROM OUR COMMANDER."

Mohamed paused for effect and purposefully looked at the players in his bus. He wondered which one of these boys would jump him if they had the slightest opportunity. He felt a shortness of breath and the sweat dripping down his face, but kept his gun pointed towards the players. Adrenalin drove him to continue.

"IF OUR DEMANDS ARE MET, YOU IN THE STANDS NEED NOT WORRY. YOU ARE MERELY THE VESSELS FOR OUR CAUSE. OUR DEMAND IS TO A LARGER AUDIENCE. HOWEVER, IF THIS DEMAND IS NOT MET, YOU WILL ALL DIE WHERE YOU SIT. BY NOW, MY MESSAGE IS BEING BROADCAST AROUND THE WORLD, SO THAT ALL CAN WITTNESS OUR COMMANDER'S DEMAND. THIS DEMAND WILL BE MADE ONLY TO YOUR PRESIDENT. WE HAVE DIVERTED YOUR TECHNOLOGY AND IF HE VALUES YOUR LIVES, HE WILL SOON APPEAR ON THE SCREEN ON THE LEFT."

Soft Target
by Larry Greer

All eyes immediately diverted from Mohamed on the right screen to the blank blue screen on the left, waiting to see if the face of President Evan White would show on that screen. Mohamed continued,

"ONLY WHEN I SEE YOUR LEADER'S FACE, WILL I COMMUNICATE MY COMMANDER'S ULTIMATUM. YOUR PRESIDENT HAS TEN MINUTES TO RESPOND."

Joe Black wondered at this man's command of the English language. He could not detect even a hint of a foreign accent. Could he possibly be an American citizen?

CHAPTER 55

The Shock

Joe Black was now rushing to his FBI office in Langley where a video conference had been set up. This was one time, he was glad he lived so close to his work. He had already contacted key members of his team to sit in on this video conference with the President. Evidently they had only ten minutes so every second counted. He was thinking, "So, *we were right after all. This was the cell that landed in New Orleans and traveled to Clemson to do whatever they are planning this evening.*"

The President was giving orders to get his key Cabinet members already dialed into the video conference. At this point, everyone was aware that time was critical in order to avoid catastrophe, whatever that might be. He directed one of the Secret Service Agents,

"Call down to the 'media outpost' at the entrance of the ranch. Get one or more network camera teams up here to the house, NOW!"

President White knew what a media nightmare this could be not only in the United States, but around the world. He would instruct the cameramen to create a "narrowcast" that would only be picked up at the Hartwell Stadium. Minutes later, the Secret Service waved the camera crew through and they bolted to the house. Something must be big to get a directive from the President. After the President told them what he wanted, each one wanted to be first to create the narrowcast. There was pandemonium among the technicians working to coordinate this narrowcast. Finally after feverish attempts, they had to tell the President a narrowcast was not possible given the 10 minute time constraint. However, they could broadcast his message, but it would be seen by the viewers around the world. The President did not want the public to have to see this live negotiation with a terrorist, but he had no option. In the meantime, the FBI, CIA Homeland Security and key Cabinet members were dialed into 'command center' screens and waiting for instructions. The President could see each of them on individual screens.

As the minutes ticked off at the stadium, the crowd, who had previously been so loud, was now whispering in subdued voices to one another. Everyone had the same question on their lips: *What could all this mean?* It was obvious to all that they were players in an event that would be part of history. And each prayed that *they* would not be listed as a fatality when history recorded it.

John Massey was agitated, but it did not appear that he could play an active part in this. He figured that he was the only person in this stadium aware of who these people were. Was this man with the black mask, the same man in the Clemson pizza restaurant he had seen several weeks back? He stared at the weapon the man was brandishing. All he had was a Glock pistol.

Larry Howard, General Manager of the stadium, had gone down to the ground level West End to investigate. Because of the soundproof nature of this floor, none of the noise from the stands could be heard down here. So, Larry did not know about the pandemonium occurring inside the stadium. He noticed that the storage room door was open and the light was on. That was out of order and he would talk to someone about this breech early next week. He peered in, but nothing seemed to be out of order, so he checked out the employee door. It had been locked from the outside. Again, this was unusual. For the first time, he began to think that maybe someone had an unauthorized key. As Larry opened the door from the inside and peered out, he noticed that there was the same small pickup truck that had been reported in the construction parking space. Now he was becoming very suspicious. He could see a note on the windshield, indicating that the driver would be back in ten minutes. He looked around and saw no one, but he did notice that there were absolutely no fans outside the stadium. That was very unusual. His gut told him that something was very wrong. Suddenly he realized that he should have been hearing fans cheering and shouting in anticipation of the start of the game. But he heard only a low buzz of what sounded like hushed voices. He checked his watch. It was 6:15pm. The game should have started at six o'clock. He ran over to one man standing at the very back of parking lot looking up at the stadium.

"What the Hell is going on?"

"Oh, my God! I was entering Tunnel B and a gunman was stopping people from coming out. I've never seen anything like this. I thank my lucky stars that I was late to the game today or I'd have been inside like all the others."

This stunned Larry and he immediately headed back towards the employee entrance. Something told him to check the truck out one more time. He saw the charcoal grill and bags of chips. That looked normal enough, But what looked strange to him were the four big ice chests that were wrapped with heavy nylon straps, securing the lids. Now, why would they need to secure an ice chest that only held drinks or food? Larry thought he had better report all this to college security.

Soft Target
by Larry Greer

CHAPTER 56

Conversations with a Terrorist

After nine minutes, there were eight Cabinet members tuned into the ranch house 'command center', including the Army Chief of Staff and the Chief of Naval Operations.
President White was sitting alone behind a table with two network cameras pointed at his face. The Presidential Seal and the American flag were displayed directly behind him. Sally sat across the table out of the view of the cameras. The technician cued the President,

"Mr. President we are ready to put you up on screen. Are you ready Sir?"

"Did we ever get the narrowcast put together or will I be broadcast to networks around the world?"

"I'm sorry Sir, still were not able to pull together a narrowcast. I'm afraid this broadcast will go worldwide."

The President glanced at Sally. "I cannot believe that we've been cornered into a conversation with some nut on live TV.

Sally responded,
"Mr. President, I know you will command the situation. Just give him rope to hang himself."

Soft Target
by Larry Greer

The technician interrupted...
"OK, THREE, TWO, ONE, WE'RE LIVE"

Instantly, The President then saw himself live on the scoreboard screen beside a man dressed all in black and wearing a mask. He was standing behind the windshield of a team bus brandishing a large machine pistol in one hand and a microphone in the other. Everyone watching the broadcast understood by now, what was going on. You could hear a pin drop, not only in the stadium, but in Pakistan and around the world as people watched this hostage situation play out on their televisions. Football fans around the country that had come to their favorite bar to watch the games, put down their glasses and stared at their President in utter silence. On the other side of the scoreboard, stood the terrorist and 15 stoic college team members. Yet again, an al Qaeda terrorist was holding America hostage. Regardless of their personal beliefs, everyone watching and everyone in the stands that day wanted to believe the President could resolve this situation without lives lost.

No American President had ever been put in a situation like this. Never had an enemy been able to bypass every level of authority and directly reach the President of the United States. What was coming next was anyone's guess.

The President decided that the first move needed to be his. Looking straight into the camera, he spoke,

"This is President Evan White. Do you have something to say to me?"

Mohamed looked up at the giant scoreboard screen. His stomach clenched as he prepared to speak to the world's most powerful leader. The ball was now in his court.

Soft Target
by Larry Greer

"I DO. I AM MOHAMED. I REPRESENT THE PEOPLE THAT YOUR COUNTRY HAS BEEN ATTACKING FOR YEARS. YOUR OPPRESSION HAS BEEN RELENTLESS ON MY PEOPLE. IT IS BECAUSE OF THIS TRYANY THAT WE ATTACKED YOUR TOWERS IN NEW YORK. YOU WOULD HAVE YOUR PEOPLE TO BELIEVE YOU HAVE DEFEATED US, BUT YOU HAVE NOT. WE ARE NOW MANY THRUGHOUT THE WORLD, AND BECAUSE OF OUR CUNNING WE REMAIN INVISIBLE TO YOU." When Mohamed stopped to make his point, The President took the opportunity to interject,

"For what purpose have you taken these innocent people hostage? What is this demand of your commander?"

"IN RETURN FOR THE SAFETY OF THESE AMERICAN INFIDELS, YOU ARE TO RELEASE TWO HUNDRED AND SEVENTY OF OUR PEOPLE AT GUANTANAMO PRISON. MY TEAM NOW IS HOLDING OVER EIGHTY THOUSAND AMERICANS HOSTAGE. IN OUR MIND THIS IS A VERY FAIR TRADE.

The President decided it was time to take control and make this personal.
"Just how do you suggest that we accomplish that?"

"YOU WILL ORDER YOUR GUARDS TO OPEN THE GATES AT GUANTANAMO PRISON. YOU WILL ARRANGE FOR THE CUBAN TV NETWORK TO SHOW US THAT OUR MEN ARE INDEED FREE. THEY ARE TO BE RELEASED INTO THE HANDS OF CUBAN GOVERNMENT OFFICIALS.

"Assuming we agree to your demands, Mohamed, it would take time. I am sure you can understand the logistics involved with getting the prisoners released and making arrangements with the

Cuban Network. I will need time to speak to my advisors. This could take hours.

Mohamed knew the President was stalling for time.
"LET ME SHOW YOU WHAT WILL HAPPEN IF YOU DO NOT AGREE TO THIS EXCHANGE.

Raga was waiting for this cue and was ready to insert the DVD.
"WE DO NOT WISH TO CAUSE THE KIND OF DESTRUCTION YOU ARE ABOUT TO SEE, BUT WE KNOW WE HAVE NOTHING TO LOSE. WE ARE AWARE THAT YOUR POLICE ARE, AT THIS MOMENT, MAKING PLANS TO ASSASINATE US AND BE ASSURED, WE WILL NOT GO DOWN ALONE."

Mohamed's face disappeared from the screen and in its place appeared a very large, well-known hotel in Las Vegas. Suddenly, there was an explosion and the hotel imploded into a cloud of dust. No one watching had to be told what this meant. They knew there was a threat of bringing the stadium down in exactly the same manner.

"WHAT YOU SAW REPRESENTS WHAT WE ARE PREPARED TO REPLICATE IF YOU RESIST OUR DEMAND. THIS STADIUM AND EVERYONE IN IT CAN BE DISINTEGRATED INTO A PILE OF RUBBLE WITH THE PRESS OF THIS BUTTON.

With that, Mohamed reached into his pocket and displayed a cell phone for the camera.

As President White digested this threat, he not only heard, but felt the panic from those trapped inside the stadium. This was a gut wrenching moment. Slowly and deliberately,

Soft Target
by Larry Greer

"We will need time to meet this demand, Mohamed." Again The President attempted to personalize the conversation.

"How much time Mohamed?" There was silence as Mohamed thought.

The President switched off the microphone and turned to address this question to his Cabinet. The Secretary of the Army was the first to speak,

"Mr. President, ask him for thirty minutes."

After a minute to consider, the others began to nod in agreement.

"Mohamed, we will need at least thirty minutes."

"NO! NO! YOU WILL HAVE TEN MINUTES. YOU WILL FIND THAT THE CUBAN TV NETWORK IS READY AT THE PRISON, AS WE SPEAK."

The President was known for making quick, effective decisions. He responded,
"We must have 20 minutes to meet your demands of hostage exchange."
Mohamed knew that the longer he gave them; the greater the odds that they would be lining up a sharp shooter to take him out. He had asked for 10 minutes, knowing that they would ask for more and he felt they could not put a sharp shooter in place sooner than 30 minutes. In addition, he had been bluffing about explosives within the stadium His only card left was the pickup truck outside the West End entrance.

"ALL RIGHT, YOU HAVE JUST TWENTY MINUTES OR THE NEXT EXPLOSION YOU EXPERIENCE, WILL NOT BE A VIDEO. AS OF THIS MOMENT, TWENTY MINUTES

Soft Target
by Larry Greer

WILL BE PUT UP ON THE SCORE BOARD CLOCK FOR EVERYONE TO WATCH THE TIME."

CHAPTER 57

Counter Point Plan

The President's microphone was killed and he could be seen moving out of camera range. People around the world watched a screen with only the Presidential Seal and total silence. It was one of the most suspenseful moments ever on live television.

Within the situation room, everyone started to talk at once. The President merely held up his hand for silence.

"Hold on a minute. I know we all have an opinion about how this should be handled, but we have only 20 minutes to act in order to prevent unnecessary deaths."
General Howard, Secretary of the Army, had served many tours in Iraq, had more experience in dealing with a terrorist attack than anyone else in the room.

"General Howard, I want to hear your thoughts."

"Mr. President, we simply cannot run the risk of underestimating this man on the bus. He speaks as if he is the leader of a team. However, at this point, we don't know how many we are dealing with. No al Qaeda cell fears death. This man is prepared to take his own life, the life of his team and heaven forbid the lives of everyone in that stadium."

The President's voice rose both in volume and tone,
"General, with all due respect, we all know what these terrorists are capable of doing. What I need from you is how in God's name are we are going to do to stop him?"

Now it was the Vice President's turn, and he addressed everyone in the room,
"Do you think it would be possible to get all cell phone providers to kill their signal towers? If he has the technology to activate any stadium explosives with that phone, shouldn't that stop his ability?"

"Not a bad idea. However, that would also keep the police and any other emergency response teams, including Homeland Security from communicating." Sally leveled.

The President then posed the question that no one had yet dared to verbalize, "Does anyone think that this Mohamed could be buffing about the explosives in the stadium?"

General Howard piped in,
"He may well be Sir, but can we afford to test him?"

The President addressed Val Simpson, Director of Homeland Security and asked him to report on the status of his team.
"Mr. President, at this time we have SWAT TEAMS from both Greenville South Carolina and Atlanta in flight. The Greenville team will be there in ten minutes. It will be about fifteen more minutes before the Atlanta team arrives. We have also been able to arrange for three platoons of Marine reservists to help secure the stadium and to remain on standby. They are already headed toward Clemson."

Soft Target
by Larry Greer

"Gentlemen, according to the clock on the wall, we now have fifteen minutes left to devise our plan. Val, what you have in the works will help in the event of a disaster but so far, I have not heard any recommendation that will AVERT this disaster. You all remember what happened on *Nine-Eleven*. This is a mad man that we are dealing with. He and his team have been trained and programmed for this very attack. I agree that we cannot afford to take a chance that he is bluffing. There are over eighty thousand American lives on the line. In less than twenty minutes they could all be buried beneath a huge pile of concrete." Evan White, now in his second term as President, knew that he would face times like this. The decision to attack Iraq was an obvious one in his mind, but he had had more than 20 minutes to make that decision.

"I have no doubt that we can release the prisoners at Guantanamo. But if we do, this man and his henchmen will still be in that stadium holding thousands of Americans hostage. Mohamed has already told us he knows we will put snipers in the stadium at the first opportunity. My fear is that they will start shooting people once we make our intentions known. This is just a damn 'catch twenty two'."

General Howard spoke up,
"Mr. President, I have advised the Guantanamo Base Commander to prepare for a release within ten minutes. All you have to do is give me the signal."

"Good General. But, I am concerned that even if we comply with his ransom demand, large numbers of people will still die in in that stadium this afternoon, once Guantanamo prisoners have been released. You might think what I am about to propose is extreme, but perhaps we need to think about deploying the 'fat boy' just as we did on Nagasaki in '45. Here is the reason I'm even thinking along these lines: It is not just these handful of men in that stadium we are up against, but the hundreds of men that trained in Pakistan or Afghanistan. I can guarantee you that they are watching this play out on the screen right now, just as millions across the world are doing. Many future terrorist actions will be determined by the success they experience in the Hartwell Stadium today. Recent events around the world have shown that once they succeed with the prisoner release, they will not stop until they pull the trigger on that stadium. Death means nothing to these terrorists. They already believe they will go to Allah's heaven tonight."

Everyone on the video conference sat in total silence as they weighed the consequences on both sides of the President's theories and proposal. Each one of them was waiting for someone else to step up to the plate. The President kept a steady gaze into the big screen. Finally without turning his head, he addressed his Secretary of Defense, Sally Robb.
"Sally, let me asks you a question? Isn't November the month the Muslims make their pilgrimages to Mecca?"

Sally took a moment to respond and finally answered,
"It is indeed. There is already millions of Muslims in Mecca or heading to Mecca as we speak."

"I think this fact plays a part in the timing of this attack. Our only choice is to smoke these people out into the open. We cannot be sure if this Mohamed is bluffing about the stadium explosives. I think our first step should be to call his bluff on that fact."

In the past year, President White had suffered from low approval ratings due to the constant questioning of, his intelligence and his leadership, and even his rights to the office, by the opposing party. Tonight, those on the conference call felt the power of both his ability to grasp a critical situation and his commanding leadership.

Soft Target
by Larry Greer

"This is our plan! Bailey, do we have a nuclear sub with a Trident Missile within a 30 minute striking distant of Mecca?" Bailey Hall was the President's Chief of Naval Operations. Before the President even finished his request, Bailey was on the line to the Navy Command Center. The President continued,

"I want this sub to have the capability of giving us every second of the live action video of this missile heading to its target. The strike we are going to make needs to be seen by our Mr. Mohamed and his cell members. I also want everyone in the stadium to experience our pre-emptive action and I want every damn terrorist to think twice about messing with American lives. If they think they have a soft target in this mission, they will think twice next time!

"OK Sally, your job is to make sure that we can see the gates at Guantanamo Prison. That needs to be broadcast within the next 5 minutes. This Mohamed character needs to think that we are making all efforts to meet his demands."

Sally made a call to the head of CNN to let them know the President's instructions. She emphasized that they needed to focus their cameras on the prison gates and within 5 minutes.

The President of CNN, who had been following this incident from his office, was already preparing to do just that. He knew a hot story when he saw one and promised Sally his team could be in place within the time required. She knew the other networks would follow CNN, in an effort to get their share points of this potential tragedy. She was now confident that whatever station was projected up on the Hartwell scoreboard would be broadcasting what was about to transpire.

Sally reported her success back to the President. During a momentary space between directives, one of the Cabinet members spoke up.

"Mr. President, with all due respect, should we not be conferring with Congress. I believe we need to get their approval for an act of war, such as this."

The President glared at this Cabinet member. And at this moment was second guessing the appointment.

"Hell, Harry, the Democrats cannot even agree on which of their deceased members they want to name a street after. The answer is NO! You need to read the Constitution a little closer. The President has the power to declare war. I would have hoped you knew that. I have my full Cabinet on this conference and I do have the right to make an executive decision. The Americans are watching and they need me to take a stand." Bailey Hall interrupted,

"Mr. President."
"Yes Bailey", he shot back a little too sharply. The idiot Cabinet member had irritated him.
"I have the Navy Operations Commander on the line. The 'Francis Scott Key' is in the Baffin Bay just off the coast of Greenland."
"Ask him how long it will take for one of his Trident Missiles to reach Mecca."
"Yes Sir." There was dead silence as Bailey listed to the Naval Operations Commander.

"Sir, the Commander says it is 5,100 miles from his sub to Mecca and at 13,300 miles per hour, it would take the missile 22.57 minutes to reach its target. Sir, it does have a satellite observation camera to observe the path of the missile."

"Bailey, tell the Commander to have the Captain of the 'Francis Scot Key' stay on the line. Order the Captain to put Mecca into his sites and be prepared to fire. I will get on the phone with him. I need to talk to him directly."

"Yes Sir," replied Bailey.

"Now, Sally, get that network on the air at the Guantanamo Prison gate. I want it up on the screen NOW."

"Yes Sir."

With one minute left on the Hartwell scoreboard, Sally stepped into the TV network room which was connected to the ranch 'command center' and directed them to put the Guantanamo live feed up on the Hartwell scoreboard. Almost immediately everyone glued to their televisions, as well as the captive fans in the stadium could see the late evening flood lights illuminating up the Guantanamo gates. It appeared that hundreds of men in white shirts and pants were standing just inside the gate. Just outside the gate, they could see Cuban soldiers poised for the release. It was obvious that the Cuban Government had known about this plan in advance.

"Mr. President, I must ask you once again, Is this really what you want to do?"

"No Harry, it is not what I want to do, but are you willing to risk all those American lives? This is not something we can debate in next Monday mornings Cabinet meeting."

"I just pray to God, Mr. President, that we are doing the right thing."

"Yes, that's a good idea Harry. You pray. We need *our* God on our side too!"

Mohamed was tense as he saw the Guantanamo gates with the prisoners standing ready to be released. He was thinking, *it is really happing, the President is going to let them go and my team and I will have succeeded.*

Sally Robb stepped in front of the camera and said "Mohamed this is Sally Robb. I am the Secretary of Defense. The President is on the phone with the Castro government and arrangements are being discussed with regards to your people's release. Please have patience and the President will be back with you in three to four minutes."

This sounded like a reasonable request and Mohamed responded.
"YOU HAVE THREE MINUTES"
The Secretary of Defense said, "Thank you, Mohamed.

The President now addresses the Captain of the submarine.
"Captain Fontain, this is the President."
"Yes Sir, Mr. President."
"Do you understand the situation, Captain?"
"Yes Sir and I have my Flag Officer, standing by awaiting my orders."
"Does our Trident missile have the range to reach its target, Captain?

"Yes Sir, it does. The target is fifty-one hundred miles which gives the missile one hundred miles to spare. It will take twenty five minutes and five seconds from firing to arrive at its destination.

"Let me ask you this Captain, and this is *very* important. If I should ask you to abort the missile with only minutes to spare, can you do that?"

"Yes Sir, I can disarm it and drop the missile into the Indian Ocean"

"Two other questions Captain Fontain. What countries will the missile fly over?"

"Sir, it will fly along the border between France and Spain and over Egypt."

"Ok, my second question is, have you worked out the logistics of patching in the view from the missiles camera to the TV network?"

"Yes Sir, my communications engineer has just worked that out and you will see the front half of the missile as she flies towards her target."

"Mr. President, I have a question I am required to ask"

"Proceed Captain."

"Sir, Protocol requires that I ask you for the Presidential secret code. I will ask Officer Miller, along with one other officer, to use their keys to open the box and see if it matches your code. This will have to be done before accepting your order to fire."

"Of course, hold on one minute." The President turned to the attaché officer and asked him to prepare to open the case. The President had a companion key on a ring in his pocket and between the two of them opened the case. The President called off the ten letters and numbers on the key and the Captain said "It's a match, Sir."

"All right Captain, please stay on the line until I get back to you."

"Yes Sir, Mr. President."

The President then turned to Sally,

"Were the networks able to come up with the two file films to supplement the missiles live picture?"

"Yes they were. I believe you want to show the one that shows the people walking around the Kaaba in the center of Mecca and then the file video of the Trident Missile being fired from a nuclear submarine. Is that correct?"

"That is correct."

The President then looked at his Cabinet for the last time. They were all staring back at him in total awe. Then the President said,

"Put me back on the camera."

CHAPTER 58

Discovery

Back at the stadium, a patrolman came up to Larry Howard,
"Don't go near that truck Larry. I'm being told that there may be something in the ice chest other than ice."

"Did you find something?"

"We checked the tag and it belongs to a Mexican that said he rented it for the day to a man who he only knows at work. He was not sure what his name was, but he did know the man was not Mexican. I do know that we have been on the lookout for Arabs, posing as Mexicans, for a couple of months now, in the Clemson area."

"What are you going to do?"
"For now we are going to put yellow tape around the area and make sure no one gets close."
"Hold on Larry, I'm getting a call."

After a one minute conversation the Patrolman said,
"Larry, I'm being told that we are to clear all people that are not in the stands out of the area. They say there is a possibility of something big."

The patrolman had been on the outside working the traffic and did not know what was going on inside. When the patrolman was out of sight, Larry took off and reentered the West End employee door.

     John Massey could only look on from their location in the stands and feeling nervous stomachs as they waited for the President to come back on the scoreboard screen. They knew that Jason was in the first bus with the lead terrorist. He was helpless to do anything to help his son. John kept feeling his gun with his fingers and wishing he was close enough to shoot this bastard. A lot of the people that had been sitting around them had moved up higher in the stands in the aisles or where ever they could think it might make a difference. John estimated that he was about forty yards away from the bus that Jason was in. If he made a dash for the bus it could only get his son and others killed. The scoreboard clock now said twenty minutes. The time was up. It was then that Sally Robb had come on and asked for three or four more minutes. To John's dismay, Molly had gotten up off the floor to see what was going on. They were both looking up at the jumbo-tron screen and could see the lights on the prisoners at Guantanamo in Cuba. Molly was crying, fearing for her son Jason.

CHAPTER 59

The Response

The President was now back on the big stadium screen. He cleared his throat and looked directly into the camera and directly into Mohamed's eyes. Then he spoke.

"Mohamed, can you see and hear me?"
Mohamed thought this was odd, but responded.
"YES AND YOUR TIME IS ABOUT UP".

"Mohamed, I'm not sure if you are bluffing about harming our people or not, but what I'm about to show you, is NO bluff."

The President then picked up his phone that had been lying on the table near him and spoke into it.

"Captain, this is the President of the United States. Do you hear me?"
"Yes Sir, I hear you loud and clear."

The Captain's voice from the 'Francis Scott Key' nuclear submarine in the Baffin Bay was on the speaker phone for all to hear. The world, at that point in time, was holding its collective breath. Everyone that could get to a TV in the past twenty minutes was watching. This included Valdess in Pakistan.

"Captain Fontain, I'm going to give you an executive order. Do you understand me?"

"Yes Mr. President I understand you."

There was now perspiration under the President's eyes, evident to all watching.

"Captain, as President of the United States, I am ordering you to fire your missile."

The Captain looked at his officer and said so that everyone could hear on the speaker phone around the world ------

"Officer Miller, I order you to fire your missile."

"Yes Sir". Officer Miller pressed his thumb against the pulsating RED BUTTON.

There was a moment of silence then the Captain came back and said,

"Mr. President, the weapon has been fired"

On clue, a technician in the network room 'command center' using a DVD projected up on the stadium screen a Trident Missile blasting from a nuclear submarine out of the ocean. It exploded water hundreds of feet into the air as it forced its way from beneath the ocean surface with ear splitting noise and belching flames as if being exorcised from the womb of a volcano.

Mohamed was frozen in place in wonderment to what was the meaning of this missile being fired before him up on the screen meant. He was silent and awaited for the President to speak again.

"Mohamed, let me explain to you what you are now looking at. This is a Trident Missile with a nuclear warhead that has eight separate parts to it and each can be fired in eight different directions. It is has the power of three point eight megatons that

Soft Target
by Larry Greer

can destroy the largest city in the world. It weighs one hundred and thirty thousand pounds and is forty four feet in length and it travels over thirteen thousand miles per hour. It is now a little under twenty two minutes from its target. Only with my command will it be diverted from its target. Do you have any questions?"

I now knew that we might have been out-smarted, but was the President bluffing or not? I still have over eighty thousand people in this stadium and as far as the President knew, I could still blow them all up. All I really had was the truck bomb outside the West End stands that I could explode and maybe cause the President to back off.

The big screen was now showing the view from the missiles mounted camera in the center of the missile focused on the direction of travel. The nose of the missile was splitting the atmosphere creating streams of white mist. Clouds could be seen fast approaching in the horizon and rapidly disappearing to its rear. It was the most captivating minutes on TV that had ever been. People in cars had pulled off the roads across the United States to listen to radios and use cell phones. No one knew where the big missile was headed, but suspected that it was heading for somewhere in the Middle East. Pakistan, India, Russia, and China had received a call from their Ambassadors saying that it was not headed their way.

The President again looking straight into the camera, spoke.
"Mohamed, you now have nineteen minutes to consider what you are doing. There is no way you or your al-Qaeda brothers can win. I recommend that you order your teammates to come down to the center of the field and lay down your weapons. You will not be harmed. You have my word on that."

I was in a sweat and could not think clearly. I was thinking that this is not the way it was planned. Did I let this man out-smart me? Right now he thinks he has the advantage, but where is that missile headed?

"YOU HAVE NOW SHOWN ME WHAT YOU INTEND TO DO, BUT NOW I WILL SHOW YOU AN EXAMPLE OF WHAT IS GOING TO HAPPEN IF YOU DO NOT ABORT YOUR MISSILE."

With that I reached for my cell phone and hit 911. The huge concrete stadium trembled in response to the earth shaking truck bomb that went off. Debris flew hundreds of feet into the air and much of the gravel from the parking lot was like shrapnel landing up in the stands and hitting people. A dust cloud, rank with the unpleasant smell of dynamite, was seen by all around the area. Fire trucks that were on standby, responded immediately, but there was no fire. Just echoes in the ears of the thousands of fans who had covered their heads in their hands. Fortunately, the police had cleared the area earlier and by some miracle no one was killed. The President was not able to see what had happened, but he could hear the explosion on his end. A technician came over to his side and reported the explosion of the truck. He let the President know that no one had been killed.

Mohamed felt like he had pulled off an effective warning signal, and had effectively frightened not only the fans, but the President.

"NOW, MR. PRESIDENT, YOU ONLY HAVE ONE MINUTE TO ABORT YOUR MISSILE."

"Mohamed, you are holding over eighty thousand people in that stadium, but now look at the big screen before you and tell me what you see?

Soft Target
by Larry Greer

I looked back up at the screen and what I saw shook me to the very core of my body. I could see thousands of people walking around the Kabba in Mecca that was the holiest of Muslim shrines. I was thinking that my family was in Mecca at that moment and I could not help but fear for their lives.

The President spoke again,
"Mohamed, you now have ten minutes left on the clock to determine if what you are doing is worth the lives of millions of your own people. Most of them are innocent of wrong doing. My people that you are now holding hostage have done neither you nor your people wrong. Do your people deserve to be destroyed because of the very act you are now threatening? Consider it. For every person you kill in that stadium, you will cause one hundred and twenty five to die at Mecca. Is that really what your Allah wants you to do?"

I knew that I had been outdone by this very clever leader. I did not have the ability to deliver on my threat. My team could kill perhaps up to one hundred people here in the stadium before being killed themselves, but was it worth it. Was I a failure or had this been a flawed plan from the beginning? Had we underestimated the power of the infidels?

President White continued,
"Mohamed, you have eight minutes to get your people down on the field and lay down their guns. My time is getting short for aborting the missile. What will it be?"
I knew what I had to do, I called out -------
"RAGA---- JOHEY---- AND THE REST OF YOU, COME AS FAST AS YOU CAN TO THE CENTER OF THE FIELD AND DROP YOUR GUNS WHERE THEY CAN SEE YOU DO IT.------ DO IT NOW!!!! DO IT NOW!!!

Soft Target
by Larry Greer

The crowds parted as the nine cell members began to run down through the stands from all the gate areas where they had held the gates closed for escape. As they jumped over the walls and down onto the field the other two from the other buses also joined them dropping their guns and headed for the center of the field. They were within minutes surrounded by armed officers.

The President who had the Captain of the 'Francis Scott Key' on the phone, told him to abort. The missile continued over its target and dropped into the Indian Ocean. No one saw it hit the water. It had been disarmed.

The only man that had not joined the other team members was still standing on the bus and still holding the microphone in his hand.

Mohamed stood there as if he was in a trance.

Jason seized his moment and charged Mohamed who still stood with the machine pistol in his right hand. The force of Jason's helmet propelled Mohamed out of the bus door and dropped him on his face with Jason landing on his back. Mohamed's training at the camp had given him well-toned muscle mass, but Jason's season of football conditioning matched Mohamed's strength. Once Mohamed recovered his breath, the two young men rolled around on the ground each struggling to get control of the pistol.

Before anyone could stop him, John Massey shot out of his seat and leapt over the wall. He sprinted onto the field with his Glock pistol, safety off and gripped tightly in his right hand. Within seconds he was standing over the two young men as they wrestled for control of Mohamed's machine pistol. Panic surged through John's body as he watched Mohamed gain control of the gun, and point it straight at Jason's head. With a purposeful calmness he aimed his pistol at Mohamed's forehead. John stared

Soft Target
by Larry Greer

deep into Mohamed's dark eyes. As their eyes locked, hatred emanated from each of their faces. In that short instant, they each realized that this was not the first time they had encountered each other. Mohamed hesitated a second too long and with a calculated aim, John Massey fired his pistol into Mohamed's forehead. Blood and brains exploded across both father and son. Still John felt no compassion for this young boy from Pakistan.

In slow motion, I saw a dark shadow move across my body and block the light. At the same instant, I could very clearly see my beloved brother Hasped, my mother and the father I revered. They were among a throng of thousands realizing their lifelong goal of worshiping Allah in Mecca. Although I had never feared for my own safety, my heart ached for my family. I could envision them at Ka'aba, the most sacred point within the most sacred Mosque.

This menacing shadow is now pointing something at me. Still, in this dream-like trance, I can see my beloved mountains above Jiba. They are clothed in the bright colors of early spring. I am sitting on a large bolder where I can keep an eye on my father's sheep. A small stream bubbles up from beneath the rocks. Its crystal clear water flows through the emerging grass, far into valley below. A cool breeze kisses my face, carrying the scent of spring flowers that cover the high mountain meadows. I remember wondering what was on the other side of those massive mountains. I have now discovered what lies outside of my sacred valley and that journey has become my fate. A moment of regret passes over me as I realize that I will never know what it is like to hold a woman in my arms or the feel of unconditional love of my own small child. As the shadow darkens over me, I wrap myself in my mother's sheepskin blanket to escape the shadow's cold breath. Feeling warm again, I close my eyes in resignation. I will never again be awakened by the deep moaning sound of the ancient sheep horn reverberating up the mountain slopes.

Soft Target
by Larry Greer

The End...or maybe not

Soft Target
by Larry Greer

Epilogue

Events within *SOFT TARGET*, weighed in heavily on real events that have taken place since 19 al-Qaida terrorists attacked the Twin Towers in New York City and the Pentagon in Washington D.C. on September 11, 2001.

Ten years after that infamous day, Osama bin Laden, at the age of fifty-four, was killed in Abbottabad, Pakistan on May 6, 2011 by U.S. Navy Seals, Team Six.

As stated in the "Warning" on the back cover of this book, it is both a work of fiction and a warning. Sleeper cells of al-Qaeda radicals may be already hiding among us or making their way to our shores.

Larry Greer
lgreer1936@charter.net

Made in the USA
Columbia, SC
23 December 2017